Without a warning...

Marissa felt strong hands clamp her shoulders and determinedly shove her far under the surface.

Before she knew it, the hands were sliding around her neck...the thumbs resting on her windpipe.

She froze, even as her pulse pounded against his fingers. This man meant to kill her!

Fear erupted into action. Her hands tried to pry his away, her legs kicked frantically, banging against his, yet driving them both upward. As they broke the surface, she caught a glimpse of his features, strong yet familiar.

She recognized it was Riley just an instant before he dragged her head forward and sealed her lips with his.

ABOUT THE AUTHOR

Dolphins have fascinated Patricia Rosemoor since she saw the movie *The Day of the Dolphin*. One of her dreams came true two years ago when she finally got close-up and personal with a small pod of dolphins in the Florida Keys. Swimming with the dolphins is an experience she'll never forget—and she's woven the tales and information obtained from their trainers or animal care specialists into this story.

Books by Patricia Rosemoor

HARLEQUIN INTRIGUE

*Quid Pro Quo trilogy

Silent Sea
Patricia Rosemoor

Harlequin Books

TORONTO • NEW YORK • LONDON
AMSTERDAM • PARIS • SYDNEY • HAMBURG
STOCKHOLM • ATHENS • TOKYO • MILAN
MADRID • WARSAW • BUDAPEST • AUCKLAND

Thanks to the organizations and individuals that
helped me obtain firsthand information on working
(and swimming) with dolphins: The Oceanarium of the
John G. Shedd Aquarium, Chicago, Illinois;
The Brookfield Zoo, Brookfield, Illinois;
Dolphin Research Center, Marathon, Florida;
Dolphins Plus, Key Largo, Florida

ISBN 0-373-22283-1

SILENT SEA

Copyright © 1994 by Patricia Pinianski

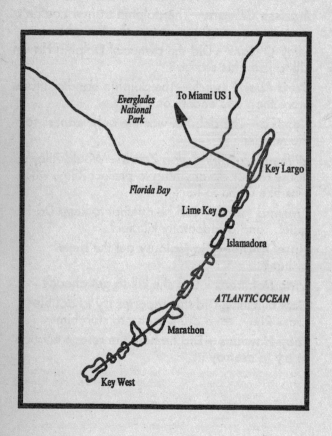

CAST OF CHARACTERS

Marissa Gilmore—The dolphin trainer couldn't identify the murderer—or so she thought.

Riley O'Hare—Did the owner of Dolphin Haven kill to keep his secrets?

Doris "Dori" Lynch—The dolphin handler made more than one enemy on Lime Key.

Kamiko—The dolphin was the only witness to the murder.

Wilhemina "Billie" Van Zandt—Would Riley's housekeeper do anything to protect Riley, who was like a son to her?

Erasmus North—Did he attempt to keep Dori quiet...and accidentally kill her?

Ansel Roche—Did jealousy get the better of him?

Vida Dahlberg—Did she kill to get ahead?

Cole Glaser—Did this reporter try to double-cross Riley...and did Dori try to stop him?

Toby Hawkins—Did he hate the refuge enough to try to destroy it?

Prologue

A wave crashed to shore and broke over Marissa Gilmore's bare feet as she raced along the sand, the steady wind whipping her long French braid between her shoulder blades. The night beach was near deserted, only a few couples lingering for a little romance under the canopy of stars.

Her own mission was desperate by comparison.

Gaze hard on the rolling Atlantic that was silvered by a bright full moon, she yelled, "Kamiko!" though her voice was already hoarse with the calling.

Still no answering clicks or squeaks. She tried not to panic. But if anything happened to the dolphin...

Her grip tightened on the mask and flippers she'd had the sense to grab before she'd started off on her search. Jack had done the same and had gone in the opposite direction. They would find her. They had to. Kamiko was *her* responsibility. Marissa's pulse lurched as she continued to jog south of the Bal Harbour Oceanarium that was perched on the sea's edge, all the while staring out past the incoming tide.

So intent was she on scanning the endless rolling expanse for some sign of the familiar silver-gray body, that she didn't realize a swimmer was riding in on the surf before her until they collided.

Stopped cold, Marissa gasped, "Sorry," as she flew off balance and fell to the pebbly wet sand, a heavy weight crashing down on her.

The swimmer was wearing scuba gear, and something sharp on the equipment had snagged her own wet suit, for the moment attaching them at the hip. Then rough hands shoved between their bodies, quickly freeing them. Without saying a word, the masked diver gathered the flippers on the sand and practically ran over her in an equal rush. Shaking her head at the rude behavior, Marissa stared for a second as the person removed the tank without slowing.

Then she stood and refocused her attention where it belonged, continuing to move south at a slower pace. She would have a few bruises in the morning. But she wasn't the important one here. Kamiko was.

How could this have happened?

A half hour ago, she'd still been waiting for the boat from Dolphin Haven to arrive. Dori Lynch, one of the marine mammal specialists from the refuge, had been late and hadn't seen fit to call in. Marissa hadn't started to worry until sunset, after the oceanarium's regular staff was gone. The assistant trainer, who'd remained on duty with her, had tried checking with the refuge, but he'd only gotten an answering machine.

And when Kamiko had begun circling the pool faster and faster, Marissa had started having this really creepy feeling. The dolphin had seemed more agitated than ever—as if she sensed she was once again being taken from her home. From Marissa. There'd been no helping it. The animal had been showing renewed signs of stress for more than a month. They'd finally elected to try another rest cure, knowing that if this didn't do the trick, the dolphin would have to be permanently retired from performing.

Now Marissa could only hope they would have the opportunity to find out whether or not some time off would help. She prayed that Kamiko, who had been born in captivity and had never had to fend for herself, would come back. For the Atlantic bottlenose dolphin had shocked even Marissa with a jump that had taken her over the retaining wall of the oceanarium's pool and straight into the Atlantic's high tide.

"Kamiko!"

Breathing hard, stopping in one spot for the moment, she followed this plea with a long blast on her training whistle. She tensed at the slight clicking sound carrying toward her on the wind.

Was that truly an answer? Or was she fooling herself?

No, there in the distance—a flash of silver curled around an incoming wave.

Pulse thudding with her rising excitement, Marissa blew the whistle again. She caught another flash of silver, but not coming for her fast and furious as she might expect. The dolphin bobbed and weaved strangely. She had no doubt that this was Kamiko—just as she was equally certain that something was wrong.

Dreading that the dolphin might have hurt herself somehow, Marissa raced through the surf. The animal bobbed and ducked and arched into the water. As they drew closer to one another, she could see Kamiko pushing at something . . . some bulky object she was propelling toward shore.

A wave hit Marissa in the knees. She bent and slipped on her flippers, turning to walk backward into the next breaker that caught her at thigh level. Pulling on her mask, she flipped forward and paddled, launching herself over a swell with huge kicks. She could barely make out flashes of the object Kamiko pushed toward her.

A minute later, she slowed and treaded water as the dolphin's burden crested on the next wave. Suddenly the thing slid into her, spinning furiously, appendages tangling around her chest and neck even as she finally got a good look....

Marissa went under, swallowing salt water and screaming into her snorkel, the choked sound one of pure horror.

For the thing that Kamiko had retrieved—the thing that threatened to drown her—was a body.

Lifeless. Eyes open and staring in a water-bloated face.

Worst of all, it was a face Marissa knew.

A face Kamiko knew.

Fighting to untangle herself from the body, fighting to get a breath of unobstructed air, Marissa understood why the boat from Dolphin Haven had been so late.

Dori Lynch would never be on time for anything again.

Chapter One

"Our dolphins really like to show off for an audience," a trainer wearing a microphone told the crowd that filled Bal Harbour Oceanarium's performance stadium. "Watch this."

Marissa was viewing the show from the upper deck. She saw the trainer give a broad sweep of her arm. The dolphin assigned to her for this show jumped, flashing its tail fluke as it arched and dived back into the pool. The audience oohed and aahed. Then another trainer slapped his open hand down on his free arm. His dolphin breached and then delivered a spectacular landing on his side—something akin to a belly flop—spraying the first few rows with water.

Happy laughter and applause filled the air.

Marissa knew the audience was captivated by the purposeful illusion of these dolphins and their larger black-and-white killer whale cousins at play in the ocean. The thick acrylic seawall blended the performing pool and the Atlantic, into which it was built, into one nearly seamless expanse.

But they'd never had an escape attempt before.

"How's it going?"

Paul Ortiz, assistant curator and head trainer since Bal Harbour Oceanarium had opened a few years before, joined her, cutting into her disturbing thoughts. His dark eyes searched her face, and she guessed he was worried about all the media attention she'd been getting since finding Dori.

She gave him a rueful smile. "Still a little numb."

"I told you to take a couple days off."

"And do what? Lie around and think about it? I'd rather work, thanks."

She'd already done one show that morning and would do another midafternoon. And in between, she'd spent some time with Kamiko, as had anyone else with a few minutes to spare.

Still not quite believing what had occurred over the past thirty-six hours, Marissa thought about the horror of dragging Dori Lynch's body to shore. A memory that would probably haunt her forever. Thank God she'd only been mildly acquainted with the woman... and that Jack had given up his own search and had come looking for her so she hadn't had to handle the trauma alone.

"Listen, Marissa, I have a favor to ask...."

Watching a demonstration of the dolphin's incredible speed below, she shrugged. "So ask."

"I'd like you to go with Kamiko to Dolphin Haven, at least until she settles in. A week. Maybe two."

Marissa took a big breath. The opportunity to spend time at a dolphin refuge should be a real thrill for her, but in this particular case, it was anything but.

"You got Riley O'Hare's permission?" she asked.

"Reluctantly."

Marissa wasn't surprised. The owner of Dolphin Haven didn't have any love for people who supposedly "exploited" marine mammals. Though she'd never met the animal rights activist herself, she'd heard enough about him to put her off. She resented the implication that her work was detrimental, rather than beneficial, to her charges.

Besides which, being at Dolphin Haven would constantly remind her of Dori.

Of being dragged under by that dead weight.

"Kamiko needs you."

Marissa flushed guiltily. Paul was right. She had to think about the animal, who was once again overstressed. Confined to the veterinary pool under the stadium, the dolphin had been in a state since they'd brought her in. The repetitive behavior that had worried them all in the first place was getting increasingly more frantic, and the vet guessed Kamiko's ulcers had returned. And, while all the trainers worked with all the animals, very often strong one-to-one bonds formed, anyway. It was that way with her and Kamiko.

"I'll do it," she agreed.

If the oceanarium had been allowed to deliver the dolphin in the first place, Dori would never have been in that boat. She might be alive now. But Riley O'Hare had insisted that his staff pick up the animal—as if trainers setting foot in Dolphin Haven would taint his holy ground.

"Good," Paul was saying. "O'Hare said the refuge's boat will be here at daybreak."

"So the oceanarium can't use its own boat even now, after everything that's happened." She shook her head. "He really is a control freak, isn't he?"

"Will that be a problem?"

"I can take it . . . on a limited basis."

Paul grinned. "If he gets too rough on you, you have my permission to give him hell."

Marissa tried to grin and failed. Normally she went out of her way to be gracious and patient. Having earned a degree in psychology, she was analytical, open-minded and usually pretty good-natured. Underneath, however, she also had a slow-building temper. Fortunately, it only popped when someone got her really riled up.

"Aren't you afraid of ruining relations with O'Hare?" she asked.

"Nah, I've known him too long," Paul said. "Besides, he has this thing about marine mammals. He would never turn away an ailing animal, no matter what his personal feelings are toward the place it came from."

This made Marissa respect Riley O'Hare even if she didn't think she would like him. "I'll do my best to work around him," she promised.

Paul's expression was grave. "I heard from Detective Lujan about half an hour ago."

At the mention of the detective in charge of the investigation into Dori's death, Marissa had trouble breathing. "What did he have to say?"

"That Dori didn't accidentally drown. The medical examiner doing the autopsy noted some bruises on her body, especially around the neck. He thinks she was choked unconscious and thrown overboard to drown."

Dori murdered. Marissa shuddered. That made everything worse. "What else did he find?"

"That the tragedy was doubled." At her puzzled expression, Paul explained, "She was a little more than two months pregnant—two lives were lost rather than just one."

"My God." Marissa wondered how many more surprises the situation held. "Do they think it was Ken Wood?"

Ken Wood was the other marine mammal specialist who had left the refuge with Dori, but who had disappeared somewhere along the way.

Paul shook his head. "He's in the clear. They stopped to gas up the boat at the south end of Miami Beach. He went for a soda, and that's the last he remembered before waking with a big headache. An employee found him gagged and tied up behind the cooler."

Marissa swallowed. "Murder. Who could have wanted Dori dead?"

"The police don't have a clue. Detective Lujan says there's a possibility of someone wanting to steal the boat, maybe to run drugs."

"The person could have knocked out Ken, not realizing Dori was aboard until it was too late." Marissa couldn't decide which was worse, being an accidental statistic or having a deadly enemy. Not wanting to continue the gruesome discussion, she said, "If I'm leaving at daybreak, I'd better start getting things in order now."

"Go to it."

After taking herself off the performance and training schedules, Marissa packed, first throwing snorkeling gear into a lightweight bag. Seeing that this was late May and that Dolphin Haven was south of the Miami area—located in the Upper Keys, Lime Key was off the highway in Florida Bay and approachable only by boat—Marissa expected her half-dozen bathing suits would be fine for the warm waters. Still, she threw in a couple of wet suits to be on the safe side.

And all the while she readied her things, Marissa thought about Dori's tragic death.

The Dolphin Haven boat had been found drifting several miles from the oceanarium, but Marissa figured it had been closer when Dori had gone overboard. She believed in the untapped intelligence and intuitiveness of marine mammals and was certain that's why Kamiko had vaulted over the retaining wall. The dolphin had sensed someone she cared about was in dire straits—Dori had taken care of Kamiko the year before at Dolphin Haven.

Throughout the centuries, there'd been hundreds of reports of dolphins saving drowning swimmers all over the world, but legend also had it that dolphins had been known to bring the bodies of drowned sailors up to shore. Which had it been in this case? she wondered. Had Kamiko thought she was saving Dori— perhaps the woman had still been alive when the dolphin had gotten to her—or had the dolphin merely brought the body in for a proper burial?

Whatever, Marissa knew the intelligent creature would remember the experience forever just as she herself would.

She only wondered if Kamiko knew more—like maybe the identity of the murderer.

THE MURDERER STARED at the front page of the *Miami Times*. The face that stared back from a curtain of dark hair was longish, attractive rather than pretty, with big pale eyes and a wide mouth.

A *big,* wide mouth.

Marissa Gilmore had been speculating about the possibility of Kamiko knowing who killed Doris Lynch. Ridiculous. The dolphin couldn't identify anyone. But Miss Know-it-all could if only she thought about it.

Running into the marine mammal trainer on the beach had been one of those twists of fate that no one could predict. Whether or not she'd told anyone about the night diver who'd knocked her flat on her fanny, the article didn't say. Maybe she hadn't thought about the incident. Yet.

But it would come to her. Eventually.

And when it did, she would be a real danger.

Unless she was taken care of first.

"WE'RE ALMOST HOME. Get ready to disembark."

At the helm of the refuge boat, Ken Wood, with a stark white bandage partly visible beneath the red curls tumbling over his neck, headed toward what looked like an island straight out of the South Seas rather than one of Florida's tiniest Keys.

So this was home to Dolphin Haven.

"My God," Marissa breathed. Despite her reservations, she couldn't help being excited by the postcard-perfect vision before them. "It's paradise."

"That's what people keep telling us." Ken grinned and his freckles seemed to dance. Despite what had happened to him, he was undeniably cheerful. "Let's hope they don't spread the word too far, or it won't be a paradise for long."

Marissa spotted several thatched peaks thrusting up beneath a canopy of tall palm trees. Two large docks, pelicans topping their pilings, anchored either end of the island. Behind one quay sat a modest, if picturesque, restaurant-bar, which also advertised a limited number of rooms for rent. To the rear of its twin dock was a badly weathered Floridian house, its crooked, screened-in balcony sweeping along the entire second floor. In between, fine white sand extended past the rocky shoreline, forming a snug beach where a lone couple took in the sun, stretched out in next to nothing on padded lounge chairs.

Ken cut the motor, and the craft drifted past the north dock and the balconied house that was set back from the water in a grove of fruit trees—mangoes, oranges and, of course, limes—toward animal pens, which had seen better days and which were built directly into the bay. Though still picturesque, the entire refuge could use some serious sprucing up.

"We have a reception committee waiting for us." Ken pointed to a couple of bottlenose dolphins peeking out of the water.

Clicks and whistles from the pens' occupants greeted them, and Kamiko, resting as comfortably as possible on deck in a stretcher specifically designed to transport dolphins, responded.

"You know you're back at Dolphin Haven, don't you?" Marissa stroked the animal's melon, the round protrusion of her forehead. "Soon you'll be in the water, playing with your old friends."

Or rather, playing where she could see her friends. For when they lowered the dolphin into the water, initially it would be into solitary confinement. Kamiko would be able to make eye contact with the refuge's occupants in the adjoining pens through the rusty chain link fencing separating them, but there would be no physical contact until she was settled in and Marissa was certain she wouldn't be further stressed by forced socialization.

The place-to-place transfer itself was stressful enough. While shaded by a canopy so her delicate hide wouldn't burn and kept wet by repeated doses of cold water, Kamiko had made the trip suspended in a sling. The transport put extra pressure on the dolphin's lungs, and it would take some time for her to readjust to another watery habitat.

"We're here," Ken said, throwing a line to a blonde who stood on the narrow wooden walkway next to an empty pen. "Vida, where's Luke?"

She quickly tied up the boat. "He's coming."

Marissa glanced past the tall blonde to see a tanned and healthy-looking dark-haired teenager fly onto the boardwalk, avoiding several rotted areas.

All the way back to the house, her eyes searched the tropical paradise, but if the owner of Dolphin Haven was aware of their presence, he was keeping that fact to himself.

RILEY O'HARE STARED OUT of the window that was slatted against the midday sun, his focus on the slim, athletic-looking woman, whose long black hair was gathered in a messy ponytail that threatened to topple off her head. She took one end of a pole supporting the sling, while his own employees took the other three, and together they guided the dolphin over the side of the boat. He should be out there, helping them, but he wasn't anxious for a face-to-face confrontation with Marissa Gilmore.

"You'll be asking her to eat with you, I expect."

As the crew used the winch to lower the sling to the water, he turned to face Billie, who'd come out of the kitchen. "I hadn't even thought about it."

"Think again then. She'll be here for a coupla weeks. You don't want her getting too nosy, digging into your business and all. Might as well get it over with."

Wilhemina Van Zandt had been Riley's house-keeper for as long as he'd been running the refuge—nearly a dozen years. Earthy, solid and crusty, Billie treated him like her own son, even though she was only approaching her mid-fifties and was barely old enough to be the mother of a man who was thirty-eight.

"You invite her, then."

He turned back to the window. The sling was in the water now, lowered by means of a pulley system sturdy enough to support the dolphin's weight. The Gilmore woman had taken charge of the release. She was meticulously careful with the dolphin's flippers and flukes, which could be hurt all too easily if improperly handled. Nearly five hundred pounds of silver-gray flesh streaked away from the sling, smoothly turned and closely circled the trainer, brushing against her affectionately before flashing off to inspect her new boundaries.

"Nice-looking," Billie commented, peering over his shoulder.

"All dolphins are," he returned, knowing the housekeeper meant the woman.

Not that Marissa Gilmore was half-bad. More to the point, she wasn't his type. They were diametrically opposed in their views of the ethical treatment of animals whose intelligence still hadn't been tested to the max.

Besides, he couldn't get Dori out of his mind. Not yet.

"You ask me, you're making a mistake if you treat her like a pariah." Billie muttered her way back into the kitchen. "Then again, you don't listen to no one when you get that hard head of yours fixed on an idea." She paused in the doorway and raised her voice slightly. "Give the girl some credit, Riley. It's obvious she loves them dolphins the same as you or she wouldn't be spending her life working with 'em. Wouldn't take much to schmooze her, keep her happy."

Riley merely grunted, knowing his housekeeper didn't expect better from him. Sometimes he expected better from himself. But not today. The dolphin's arrival added salt to a fresh wound. He'd been through with Dori months ago as a result of her betrayal. That his former lover had to die was one thing. But the death of the unborn child that he hadn't even known about—the child who might very well have been his own flesh and blood—was another.

Staring blindly in the direction of the pens, trying to decide whether or not he had the guts to show up at Dori's funeral the next day, Riley wondered if he would ever be able to forgive himself.

"LIKE SOME COMPANY?"

Marissa looked up from her evening meal, a piece of grilled swordfish floating in a red- and yellow-pepper sauce. "Are you O'Hare?" she asked, disappointed by this boyish-looking, sandy-haired man.

Somehow she'd imagined Riley O'Hare to be more...
impressive.

Thick eyebrows flashed up over hazel eyes, the
stranger's most attractive feature. "Me? You've got to
be kidding. Name's Cole Glaser." He hesitated, then
added, "I'm a guest at the resort."

"I'm not." Oddly enough, her disappointment dissipated, while her frustration at not having met the
master of the refuge was refueled.

"I thought you had the cabin farthest back in our
little private jungle."

Had he been watching her? Telling herself his interest was undoubtedly innocent, Marissa nevertheless said, "I'm here to work, not socialize," perhaps
a bit too abruptly. "And I'll be heading back to work
in another few minutes... as soon as I finish eating."

Getting her drift that she wanted to be left alone,
Glaser backed off. "Another time, then." He chose a
table several away from Marissa's, yet he took the seat
directly facing her.

While on Lime Key, she was, indeed, staying at the
Lime Tree Resort. Resort was a bit of an exaggeration, since the retreat consisted only of the dock, the
restaurant-bar with some second-floor rooms for rent,
a water-sports equipment shack and a dozen individual thatch-roofed suites.

As Glaser had pointed out, her own quarters were
the farthest from the dock area, with an abundance of
vegetation surrounding it, giving her maximum privacy. She couldn't even see another building. The interior was decorated with rattan furniture and had a
palmetto ceiling, while the outdoor shower was
screened by bamboo poles. Comfortable, if simple.

The resort had a laid-back charm Marissa truly appreciated. And the food was wonderful. Among the crowd of diners, many of whom had come over from one of the other Keys, was the couple who'd been on the beach and, of course, Cole Glaser, who kept giving her inquisitive looks.

A deep voice cut through her thoughts. "Is your meal satisfactory?" Ansel Roche, the fortyish owner of the tiny resort, stood at her table.

"Marvelous. Quite a treat considering my own simple culinary skills," Marissa admitted.

Normally she bought deli food or grilled a piece of fish or chicken breast and made herself a salad. Not cooking simplified a life already complicated by her particularly demanding work.

As if he realized that, Ansel said, "But you possess skills that are far more important than wielding a skillet."

Marissa smiled at the attractive man whose chiseled features were complemented by dark blond hair, a flawless tan and a fit six-foot frame encased in island white slacks and shirt. If he was trying to score points with her, he certainly was succeeding. She appreciated anyone who appreciated her work.

"So are you a dolphin aficionado?" she asked.

"From a distance."

Thinking that the entrance to the refuge was barely a hundred yards across the small beach, she said, "But you're so close—"

"But not to Riley O'Hare." Ansel's tone changed to contempt when he uttered the name. "The owner of Dolphin Haven is damn protective of his preserve. He doesn't like poachers."

Before Marissa could ask him to explain the odd statement, the door opened and another couple entered. Ansel's tense expression relaxed.

"If you'll excuse me?"

"Of course."

Finishing her dinner, Marissa wondered again about the enigmatic owner of Dolphin Haven. He'd made no effort to meet her when they'd brought Kamiko in, and yet she'd sensed his presence as if he was aware of her every movement. Was he really the ogre various people made him out to be? Other than his caring for marine mammals, Riley O'Hare didn't seem to have anything else in his favor.

She was still thinking about the situation when, after signing her bill, she headed for the refuge intending to check on Kamiko.

The refuge had four good-size pens sunk directly into the water of the bay. Earlier that day, Marissa had gotten Kamiko settled into the isolation pen. A second pen held an adult male and his harem of three females. A third was home to two juvenile females and a juvenile male, while a fourth housed one pregnant female and another female with a nursing calf that was nearly a year old. The pens were interconnected both underwater, with trapdoors so the dolphins could be moved around, and above water, with plank walkways for the workers.

The sun was setting, and she had to strain to see the dolphin skimming the bottom of her pool, belly-up. Once Kamiko realized her trainer was there, however, she whistled in greeting and zoomed through the water, stopping abruptly mere inches from where Marissa was kneeling.

"Hey there, sweet girl, how are you?"

Kamiko tilted her head and inspected Marissa with one eye. She made a series of clicking sounds. In response, Marissa used sign language, turning her hand from palm down to palm up in a smooth gesture that indicated the dolphin should turn over and float on her side.

When she did, Marissa stroked the smooth, rubberlike skin that was far more delicate than it appeared. As did all dolphins, Kamiko had various rake marks scarring her body, some from the teeth of other dolphins trying to show their dominance or irritation, others simply from her trying to scratch an itch on some rough, rocky surface. Enjoying the petting, Kamiko continued to talk to Marissa in clicks and squeaks. Marissa signaled the dolphin to present her head, mouth open, then she scratched the animal's sensitive tongue, one of Kamiko's favorite treats.

When she took her hand away, however, Kamiko quickly dipped, then raised her head and spit water all over Marissa.

"Hey, you!" Laughing, Marissa splashed back.

The dolphin deluged her again.

"You want to play, do you?"

Delighted that the dolphin had relaxed enough to want to play, Marissa couldn't help herself. Grabbing a nearby plastic ring—one of many dolphin-safe toys around—she pitched it as far across the pen as she could. Kamiko was after it in a silver flash. Then, having kicked off her sandals, Marissa dived into the pen after the animal, mindless of her white shorts and blouse.

What followed was a one-sided game of keep away, the dolphin keeping the plastic ring away from the human and having great fun in doing so. Kamiko would let Marissa get within inches of the toy before launching herself and the ring to the other side of the pool—the noises she made sounding very much like a teasing laugh.

"Okay, I give up," Marissa finally puffed, throwing her arms up to show her surrender.

Kamiko glided across the pool and presented the ring encircling her bottle-slim snout. Marissa lifted the toy, then kissed the tip of Kamiko's nose. Latching onto the dolphin's dorsal fin, she was taken on a speedy tour. As they neared the connecting pens, other dolphins greeted them, each signature whistle distinct from the next.

She couldn't see much in the dark except moonbeams bouncing off the calm water's surface and a few slick, silvered backs . . . and a dusky silhouette frozen amidst several palm trees at the edge of the pen.

Gasping in surprise, Marissa let go of Kamiko and took in a mouthful of salty seawater. She stared into the dark, waiting for the unknown person to identify himself. For it was a man, tall and well muscled. That much she could gather from the haze of moonlight ringing him.

Underwater, Kamiko nudged her legs, but Marissa ignored the further invitation to play. The man had to know she saw him, but still he did not declare himself. Why not? What did he think he was up to? She glared into the dark, and as if he sensed her annoyance, the stranger started to back off.

"Not so fast!" she called, swimming furiously the few yards to the boardwalk before he could disappear on her. "The least you could do is identify yourself!"

He stopped and stared in silence, and a chill ran up her spine. Still, she wasn't about to back down. She was boosting herself up onto the wooden planks of the walkway, when he finally said, "Riley O'Hare."

"I should have known." Her simple statement held a wealth of meanings, and he could damn well choose whichever one he wanted. After getting to her feet, she demanded, "Why didn't you say something?"

"I didn't want to disturb you." His voice was deep. Mellifluous. "Or the dolphin."

Ignoring her primal physical response to his smooth tone, Marissa glanced back into the pen. Kamiko hung around nearby, head cocked as if trying to assess the situation for herself.

"Or maybe you didn't want me to disturb you," she finally said, turning back to the owner of Dolphin Haven.

"What?"

"I know you're not a fan. That's okay. I appreciate your concern for my dolphin."

"She's not yours."

"The oceanarium's then."

"She belongs to herself. You merely hold her captive."

An old argument, but one Marissa was used to. "She was born in captivity. She doesn't know anything else." And she couldn't help but issue a challenge in return. "What about the dolphins *you* keep?"

"I don't presume to own them."

"Yet they, too, are captive."

He moved closer, and the first thing she noticed was that Riley O'Hare was a few inches over six feet; the next was that he seemed to be nude.

Actually, he was clad in a bathing suit, the brief, pale garment revealing a broad chest and muscular thighs among other positive male attributes. He was

large and athletically fit enough to be intimidating.
Only she didn't intimidate easily. She stared up into
the crags of his shadowed features beneath a wave of
dark hair. What she could see of his expression was as
hard as she imagined his body to be.

"Some of the dolphins here are castoffs of shows
and wouldn't know how to survive in the wild themselves anymore," he said. "While we let them swim in
the bay in the hope that they'll take off with a pod,
they always return to what they were taught to know.
Three of them were beached and sick. We nursed them
back to health and will attempt to set them free soon.
Another, like yours, is here for a rest cure and will go
back to jail when the vet says she's cured. If there is a
cure for heartsickness."

Behind her, Kamiko whistled and clicked, the lonesome sounds punctuating O'Hare's statement. But
Marissa knew that if she thought of her charges'
homes as jails or of their being heartsick for the wild,
she couldn't do her job properly.

And she definitely didn't want to argue. "Well, I'm
glad I finally got to meet you, Mr. O'Hare."

"You might be sorry before it's time for you to
leave, so don't get too comfortable."

Was that a threat? she thought.

The wind whispered through the palms, the fingers
of air making her wet flesh rise.

"I'm not here for my own pleasure," she told him,
slicking back her dripping hair. "I wouldn't even be
here if Dori Lynch hadn't had that accident."

"Dori didn't have an accident. She was murdered."

He said it so coldly, so matter-of-factly, that he
might have been speaking of a stranger rather than

someone who'd been working closely with him for several years.

"Yes, well—"

"The police have no clues except for what *you* saw," he stated.

"I didn't see anything."

"You found her."

"Not me. Kamiko."

When he didn't respond, Marissa realized he was staring at her. His gaze flicked away from her face. Lower. Glancing down, she realized the moonlight was illuminating her white blouse, wet and perfectly molded to her braless breasts, and her nipples were pebbled against the cool material. Flushing, she crossed her arms over her chest.

As if he hadn't broken the conversation with his rude stare, Riley said, "Nevertheless, take care, Miss Gilmore. Don't go wandering around the Key alone at night."

"If you don't want me down here alone with the dolphins, then just say so."

He didn't. "And make sure your door is locked tight."

Not a threat exactly, but a warning, one that put her back up. "I'll be careful," she promised, "though wandering around a half-wild Key at night couldn't possibly be as dangerous as Miami at any hour."

He didn't smile at her attempted humor.

Realizing he was waiting for something—for her to leave?—she slipped into her sandals, gave Kamiko one last pat and headed for the gravel path that would lead her to the interior of the small island where her cozy quarters awaited. She had one difficult moment—she had to maneuver by him on the walkway and was determined not to touch him. Though she succeeded, her flesh rose with goose bumps, making her feel as if he'd touched her all over.

Only when she was out of the fenced area did she allow herself to glance back.

Seeming to have forgotten her existence already, the owner of Dolphin Haven had moved past the isolation pen to the largest enclosure holding the four adult animals. Half-silvered in moonlight, with sleek dolphins gathering excitedly in a semicircle around him, he looked like an ancient god wielding power over magical creatures.

He dived, his powerful body a flawless line as he cut smoothly into the dark water. When he shot back up, it was between two dolphins who lifted him into a perfect arc as they dived again, taking him with them.

Reminded of a Greek statue she'd once seen—Eros riding a dolphin at Aphrodite's side—Marissa flushed for a second time, embarrassed now by her own wayward thoughts, for he stirred her sexually against her will.

She let anger burn away the shame.

Riley O'Hare had been trying to scare her off his turf, since his obvious intent was to have the dolphin pens all to himself at night. So why couldn't he have been more direct? And why did she feel like looking over her shoulder all the way back to the cabin?

She had nothing to fear.

Only the silent sea stood testimony to Dori Lynch's murderer.

Chapter Two

The Gilmore woman defied all logic. She'd walked right into the viper's nest with no thought to her own safety. Fevered eyes stared at the thatch-roofed cabin as though they could see through the thin walls to the occupant within. No doubt she was sleeping.

Vulnerable.

How easy it would be to creep right in and snuff out the only possibility of exposure....

Marissa Gilmore was either incredibly brave or downright stupid. Or perhaps she was simply naive and had no idea of the danger that awaited her.

As dawn broke over Lime Key, she doubtless remained snug in her bed, comforted by her own self-righteousness and an inflated sense of self-worth. She was here to do her humane best with her precious dolphin, not to find a killer.

Or was she?

If the latter was her purpose, then they were of the same mind. The sooner the better.

Afterward, though...

Only one of them would survive to tell the tale, and there was no lack of certainty as to which one of them that might be.

With the Gilmore woman silenced forever, no one would ever know.

AFTER A FITFUL night's sleep filled with strange, erotic dreams—very likely conjured up by a certain moonlit apparition—Marissa forced herself out of bed when the alarm rang at six.

A quick spray in the outdoor shower woke her, and she climbed into a turquoise bathing suit and a matching thigh-length net cover-up before shooting over to Dolphin Haven, where breakfast awaited everyone who worked on the refuge. Ken Wood had told her that both morning and midday meals were supplied so they could all share information about the animals while they ate, rather than take up precious time with regularly scheduled meetings during the day.

Despite Riley O'Hare's altruism about not using marine mammals for entertainment purposes, he and his employees did do research with some of their intelligent charges.

"It makes sense, his going to the funeral," a raspy voice was saying as Marissa approached the deck at the back of the house where she'd been told meals would be served. "He was involved with her for quite a spell."

The mention of the funeral made Marissa stop dead in her tracks. Made her remember Dori's water-bloated face and staring eyes. A deep breath dispelled the vision that continued to haunt her.

Nearly as shabby as the old house, the newer deck was up several steps, between the floors. A man who looked to be about sixty was at the rail swigging a cup of coffee with Billie Van Zandt, the housekeeper. They could almost be a couple, Marissa thought, so at ease did they seem with one another. While Billie was solid and tough-looking, the man was stocky and grizzled.

"Riley never should have gotten involved with Dori in the first place," came Billie's reply. "She was all wrong for him. Untrustworthy."

Vida Dalberg crossed to a long built-in counter filled with breakfast items, saying, "That didn't stop her from letting Riley knock her up."

An appalled silence was followed by a heated "Riley didn't knock anyone up!"

Though she couldn't see him from where she stood under a palm tree along the path, Marissa recognized the voice of Luke Strong, the teenager who'd helped with Kamiko's release the day before. She considered the accusation. The coroner's report had mentioned the pregnancy but, of course, hadn't guessed at the paternity.

"Okay, okay," Vida said, sounding annoyed as she loaded a plate with fruit. "Don't throw a hissy fit. I don't know why you'd care, anyway."

"Maybe the boy just don't like your trashy mouth," the grizzled man said.

"Oh . . . stuff it, Erasmus!"

Not knowing what to do, Marissa stood frozen, hoping the conversation would settle down to something more amicable before she intruded. But the stocky stranger's gaze was sharp and found her amidst the palm trees.

"Who's this?"

Stepping forward, she introduced herself. "Marissa Gilmore." Now that she'd been spotted, she ascended the steps quickly, as if that had been her intention all along. "I'm a trainer at Bal Harbour Oceanarium."

"Ah, you brought in the sick dolphin."

He obviously knew who she was.

"Name's Erasmus North," he went on. "Fisherman. I supply this place with a fresh catch of dolphin chow every morning, seven days a week."

"Then you work here, too."

"Nope. Work for myself. Riley O'Hare happens to be my best customer, has been for the better part of the dozen years he's been running this place."

Undoubtedly that's why Erasmus seemed so much at home, helping himself to another cup of coffee, sitting on a chair this time and propping his feet up on the rail. Meanwhile Billie slipped back up the few steps into the kitchen, and Luke sullenly stuffed his mouth, his vivid green eyes glaring at Vida, who sat across the table from him.

After pouring herself a cup of coffee, Marissa took a swig, then prepared herself a bowl of granola with sliced banana. "Is Ken down by the pens?" She was counting on him to run her through the shelter's rules and regulations first thing. She didn't need Riley O'Hare on her back again.

"Kenny went to the funeral with Riley," Vida said, popping a chunk of fresh pineapple into her mouth.

Marissa wondered why the blonde hadn't gone, too. Then again, from the sound of her earlier barb, Dori and she probably hadn't been fast friends.

Minding her own business, she set about the task of eating breakfast. Erasmus soon left for the dock and his boat, and Vida entered the house. Finished with her cereal, Marissa returned to the food counter for more coffee and a muffin. Vida's voice drifted out from the kitchen.

"Billie, Kenny said Riley made some calls to a couple of aquariums."

"Maybe he did."

"But why, when I'm here?"

"You'll have to take that up with him."

"Can't you put in a good word for me?" the blonde wheedled as Marissa returned to the table. "You know how long I've been waiting for this chance."

"Riley has his own mind."

"But you help him make important decisions."

"Not about the dolphins."

"Then you won't help me?"

"If Riley thinks you're right for the job," Billie said stiffly, "he'll offer it to you."

"Terrific!"

Vida slammed out of the kitchen, her long legs tearing down the steps of the deck. The blonde didn't say a word to Marissa, and her drop-dead gorgeous looks were spoiled by the anger clearly tensing her features. Luke continued to eat in silence, sunglasses now covering his eyes. It wasn't until Marissa had finished her meal and was on her way to check on Kamiko that the teenager decided to get friendly.

"Wait up, Marissa," he shouted, jogging to catch up with her on the path.

She waited and wondered. How did someone as young as Luke Strong fit into Dolphin Haven?

"Vida wants Dori's job and'll do practically anything to get it," he told her without preamble.

So she'd gathered from Vida's exchange with Billie—but why did Luke choose to discuss the situation with *her?*

"Yesterday, I had the impression she was one of the marine mammal specialists," Marissa said.

"Nope. Normally she gives paid tours to visitors and sells them souvenirs to raise money for the refuge. She sends out mailings for contributions, too. And Riley lets her do the grunt work. Ordering supplies. Clean up. Stuff like that. She only gets to work with the dolphins when we're really shorthanded, like now."

"But *you* work with them? No offense." She stared at the young face half-hidden by sunglasses and a curly mop of dark hair brushing his forehead. "Maybe you're older than you look."

"Seventeen." At her raised brows, he shrugged and added, "I was practically born in the water, and I've been close to dolphins most of my life. Besides, the owner's son *should* get special privileges."

Having dropped that bombshell, Luke jogged past Marissa and kept going until he reached the pen holding the juveniles. Without hesitation, he jumped in, creating a big splash. One of the young dolphins breached, as well. A teenager playing with a teenager.

Appropriate.

So Luke was Riley's son. The different last names had fooled her, of course, not to mention that Luke didn't call Riley Dad. Had Luke been adopted by a stepfather? From his reputation alone, Riley O'Hare didn't seem like the type of man to give up anything that was his, especially not a son. Maybe he'd never married the kid's mother and Strong was her maiden name.

That thought led her back to Vida's comment about Riley being the father of Dori's baby... and the fact that Luke had gotten so hot over it. Whether or not Riley had been responsible, he had been having an affair with Dori, that much was clear. So how could he have been so cold the night before when the subject of her death had come up?

Though her own treasure-seeking father had been irresponsible to his own family members when he'd been on a hunt, he'd never seemed disaffected toward them.

Shaking away thoughts of Riley O'Hare that didn't directly concern her, Marissa focused on the creature that did. Having been alone for one night, Kamiko had returned to a repetitive behavior pattern. Ignoring the dolphin-safe plastic toys in the water—the hoop from last night and a ball—the dolphin was swimming across one short corner of her pen, somersaulting at the chain link fence, swimming back to the start, somersaulting again and then crossing back without so much as hesitating.

Marissa knelt at the edge of the pen and splashed water with both hands to get the dolphin's attention. While she was certain that Kamiko had sensed her presence long before she'd signaled it, the dolphin refused to break her concentration. Marissa sighed. Things weren't going to be as easy as she'd hoped.

Removing her cover-up, she dropped it onto the deck and dived into the pen where she swam in the same pattern as the dolphin. Eventually Kamiko gave in and broke off the monotonous game, circling Marissa and rubbing up against her.

In return, Marissa ran her hands affectionately along the dolphin's sides and made a silent promise to concentrate on *her* needs—like getting a dose of Pepto-Bismol into Kamiko's stomach to calm any irritation—and to put the enigmatic owner of Dolphin Haven out of her mind.

RILEY O'HARE DIDN'T return to Lime Key until after the sun had set. His boat pulled up to the Dolphin Haven dock just as Marissa finished another lone gourmet meal at the resort. Through the restaurant's wall of screened windows, she watched him disembark, tie up the boat and confer with Ken as they headed for the house. Throughout dinner, *her* every move had been monitored by that sandy-haired Cole Glaser, whose sharp too-interested gaze made Marissa glad to be free of the place.

She was determined to check on Kamiko whether the refuge's owner liked it or not. He hadn't actually said she *couldn't* wander around the premises at night. Only that she shouldn't.

Still, she slipped around back, avoiding the house itself and approaching the pens from the rear path through the undergrowth. She had just passed the refuge's boundary fence when a shadow suddenly glided stealthily alongside her, making her jump, then stop dead in her tracks. Dressed in black, he practically blended in with the night.

Heart pounding, much to her annoyance, Marissa tried to speak as if unaffected by his sudden arrival. "Do you ever announce yourself?" she asked the owner of Dolphin Haven.

He answered with a query of his own. "You have a penchant for disregarding warnings, don't you?"

He stepped closer. Too close. His potency was palpable. Her flesh responded to an unspoken invitation. Her pulse shuddered through her and her mouth went dry. Though she wanted to, she refused to step back.

"I've been known to buck the system and frustrate some people." Especially control freaks, she thought, though she didn't say so. "But I never do it lightly. If Kamiko hadn't been all wound up again today, I wouldn't feel it necessary to go against your wishes."

"I was only thinking of your safety."

He'd been drinking. She caught a hint of alcohol on his breath when he leaned in closer. As a matter of fact, she suspected he might be a little drunk. Not that he was weaving. He wasn't even slurring his words. More noticeably, there was a mellowness about him that she hadn't seen the evening before. He was almost... pleasant... enough to be dangerous.

"Death isn't pleasant," he pronounced as if reading her mind.

"I didn't think it was."

"Especially not when the person being buried is someone you know." His gaze bored into her when he asked, "How well did you know Dori?"

Having trouble breathing normally at his very nearness—at the way he seemed to be prying inside her—she shook her head. "We'd met a few times, starting when she picked up Kamiko from the oceanarium last year." Though he wasn't touching her, she swore she could sense the warmth of his flesh. "Then again at a conference in Orlando this winter. Mostly we talked about the Marine Mammal Protection Act. And Kamiko's progress. I didn't really get to know Dori personally."

Though even now she could see the dead woman in her mind's eye. Could feel Dori's body tangling around her own.

Pushing her under...

The grim vision dispelled the sensual effect he had on her.

"I knew Dori as well as one person can know another," he was saying, "and still not know them at all."

Surprised at his making the admission to her—a total stranger—and wondering at the lack of emotion he expressed, considering the woman had been his lover, she found herself challenging him. "Then you must be hurting." She didn't try to hide the irony she was feeling.

But he must have missed it, because he said, "Mostly I feel empty." Indeed, even sounding hollow, he added, "As if I'm removed from the situation. What about you?"

An invisible weight pressed down on her, and she was swallowing salt water again. "I don't really want to talk about it," she said in an effort to dispel the horrible feeling of helplessness that had nearly paralyzed her out in the ocean.

"Why not?" he asked. "It's good for the soul."

"Confession is."

"What?"

"Confession is good for the soul." Her tone light and inviting, she offered up the old platitude that usually had some validity. "Maybe it's you who needs to do the talking."

"You mean I should be confessing." The emptiness was instantly replaced with anger. "I'd be very careful about making accusations, if I were you."

She blinked. She hadn't meant her statement the way he'd taken it. She'd been thinking of his ill-fated relationship with Dori—and of the child—not of the murder. Why was he so touchy?

Did he have reason to be?

She stared at him and wondered....

"What *did* you see that night?" he demanded, his voice soft, yet somehow menacing.

She sucked in a lungful of humid air. "I told you—nothing."

"But you were there!"

Alarmed by his vehemence and the way he was looming over her, she swallowed hard and stepped back. "I was out searching for Kamiko. As I told the police, she's the one who found Dori. Maybe she saw something I didn't." A nervous laugh escaped her. "Of course, getting a dolphin to talk isn't the easiest thing in the world now, is it?"

"Sometimes it's possible . . . if you know how."

And as smoothly and as silently as he'd appeared, he backed off, quickly vanishing into a stand of palms opposite the pens. He was there one second . . . gone the next.

Marissa was left feeling mildly stunned by the strange encounter. She shivered and rubbed at the gooseflesh on her arms. Riley O'Hare really was an odd one.

The question was . . . was he also dangerous?

Her imagination was getting the better of her. He was a man upset by a former lover's death and trying not to show it, that's all. A former lover and a child that would never be born.

It had nothing to do with her.

Not wanting to think about it any longer, Marissa did what she had come to do. She checked on Kamiko.

Relieved to find the dolphin spying on her neighbors through the chain link fencing—the two females and the calf, who seemed equally curious—she quietly watched and listened to their exchange of clicks and squeaks.

What kind of conversations did dolphins have? she wondered. Could Kamiko be telling her new neighbors about the shocking events surrounding their caretaker's death?

Perhaps a quarter of an hour slipped by before she remobilized. On the way back to her cabin, she looked in vain for some sign of Riley O'Hare and told herself she was not disappointed. Still, she felt as if unseen eyes were following her as she made her way to her quarters.

Could he be lurking about, watching her?

The thought renewed her goose bumps and lent speed to her feet. She was relieved to enter her cabin, alone and safe, though the place felt rather stuffy. No wonder—the ceiling fan wasn't turning. Though she didn't remember doing so, she must have shut it off earlier. Switching it back on, she also opened some windows to catch the cross breeze, muggy as it might be. Lime Tree Resort was too primitive for air-conditioning.

Though she'd cleaned up before going to dinner, the heavy humidity made her feel grubby, so she opted for another shower. Might as well feel clean and cool before trying to sleep. After changing into a gauze cover-up and grabbing a bath towel, she moved to the outside stall of bamboo that barely came to her shoulders. A single dim bulb lit the enclosure with its wood-slat floor. She left her towel hanging on the outside of the door, which banged shut behind her. Then she removed the filmy cover-up and, after opening the door a crack, secured it on the hook next to the towel.

The initial spray of water was a shock. Cursing herself for not being more cautious, she jumped back from the cold stream. Her foot tangled with something soft and wet. She glanced down. Her washcloth. She usually draped it over the shower handles to dry, so how did it get on the floor on the opposite side of the cubicle?

As soon as the water warmed, she bent over to snatch up the washcloth. An unexpected weight gave way, and when she looked back down, she saw a slight movement in the shadows. She made a face. Probably some small rodent or very large palmetto bug had made itself comfortable under the damp terry cloth. With an even bigger grimace, she flung the washcloth over the shower handle—she really didn't need to do anything but rinse off a little sweat, anyway.

The water was feeling good now, and Marissa stepped forward, ducking under the stream and flooding her face and loose hair. A soft noise was distorted by the beat of water against her head, so she drew back a minute and listened.

Nothing.

Still, her pulse escalated just a little, and she remained on the alert as she ducked back under the water. Just when she thought she'd been imagining things, there it came again. Drawing back, she strained to listen, picking up a soft, slithering sound that made her breath catch in her throat.

The sound was close. Too close. At her feet.

Not at . . . on.

Marissa swallowed hard.

Something stopped her from jumping and screaming. Something made her look down through her wet curtain of hair very carefully first.

A thin, nearly two-foot-long reptile was wending its way over her foot.

A red and black and yellow snake.

Dear God, was it a deadly coral snake or a scarlet snake, an innocuous look-alike?

The serpent was now stretched across both her feet, luxuriating in the "rain" provided by the shower. If she should move, a coral snake would surely see that as a threat and clamp onto her flesh—probably one of her toes, for it had a small mouth—and inject its deadly poison. Marissa had heard it called a twenty-minute snake because it could shut down a person's respiratory and nervous systems that fast. The mortality rate was too high for comfort.

Her mind whirled as the serpent continued to drape itself over her flesh as if it had no intentions of leaving. Forcing herself to remain still and silent—except for the breathing she couldn't control—she conjured up the old rhyme of her childhood: *red on yellow, kill a fellow... red on black, venom lack.*

The bare bulb over the shower revealed yellow bordering big bands of black, separating the black from the red. Definitely a coral snake.

Death in a pretty package.

A breath shuddered through her and her knees grew weak. What the hell was she supposed to do now? Not panic, that was for certain. Panic could mean her death.

She had to think.

Coral snakes liked the rain. This one certainly did. That she could do something about. Moving ever so slowly so as not to alert the reptile, she reached out with both hands, clasped the shower handles and shut down the water a little bit at a time.

The "rain" stopped but still the snake didn't budge.

"Come on," she whispered. "Go someplace else. There's a nice puddle of water over there."

As she waited for the snake to leave, she heard another sound outside the shower, like someone traipsing through the undergrowth. Should she shout for help? Or would involving another person at this point make things worse?

Before she could decide, the coral snake made up its mind and began slithering off her foot. Marissa reached for the door and readied herself to jump out of the shower, only hoping she would be faster than the reptile.

Slow it down.

Heart pounding, she slid her hand over the door just as the thought came to her. She clutched the gauze cover-up, and watching the snake move toward the puddle, she carefully hauled the material into the shower.

The person outside was coming closer. The sound of light footsteps directly on the path . . .

The tail end of the coral snake slid off her. Waiting barely a second longer, Marissa dropped the gauze over the reptile at the same time as she lunged against the door.

The wood panel swung open, and she flew into a solid body.

Naked, wet and weak with relief, hair dripping all over his black shirt, Marissa looked up into the glowering expression of Riley O'Hare.

Chapter Three

"What the hell is going on?" Riley demanded.

"S-snake..."

Shock was setting in, so Marissa could hardly speak. She clung to Riley's warmth for all she was worth. Her legs were shaking along with the rest of her, and she feared she would fall if she let go.

"There's a snake in your shower?"

She could only nod in response, fat droplets of water from her hair hitting him in the face.

"Probably harmless," he growled, looking at her as if she was just some naive, hysterical female.

"N-no. C-coral snake!"

He drew her farther back from the shower stall as he asked, "Are you certain you know a coral snake from a—"

She punctuated her vehement "Yes!" with an even more vigorous nod, virtually deluging him.

"Damn!" He set her away from him, ignoring the water dripping down his cheeks. "Stay put and keep your eyes open in case it crawls this way."

Riley made a quick inspection of the grounds, finally picking up some gardening tools that had been left lying around the side of her building. Seemingly unaware of the fact that she was standing in front of her cabin stark naked, he advanced on the shower stall, rake in one hand, giant bush cutters in the other. Despite his order, Marissa followed close behind, taking the opportunity to whip her towel from its hook as he grasped the handle of the door.

He paused long enough to say, "You haven't got anything I haven't seen before—now get the hell back!" And then he swept the door open.

No fool, Marissa edged away as she secured the towel around her. "Under the material," she cautioned.

The door was half-closed, so she couldn't quite see what Riley was doing. But she heard his satisfied "Got it," followed by the metallic snip of the giant shears.

She didn't need to see it to get the picture. Added to the terror she'd experienced, this was too much for her system. Her stomach revolted, and she hunched over the arrowhead plants opposite her front door, where she quickly regurgitated her dinner. When she straightened, Riley was standing in the shower-stall doorway, staring at her.

"Quick thinking." When she gave him a blank look, he added, "Throwing your cover-up over the snake." He moved toward her. "Let's get you inside."

Before he could put his hands on her, Marissa made for the door. Having moved past embarrassed right on to humiliated, she couldn't look him in the eye.

And so when she stepped inside and realized he was directly behind her, she turned and stared somewhere in the region of his knees. "Thanks."

"I'm not done."

Her forehead creased in mild irritation, she glanced up at his expression, which had turned neutral. "You don't have to hold my hand."

"I thought I'd take a look around. Make certain your visitor didn't have a friend."

Considering that possibility, she couldn't swallow. But she did let Riley in. She stood in the middle of the room while he checked all the nooks and crannies. He even gave the closet and the space under her bed a once-over. The ceiling fan was directly overhead, its sweep of air now making her body shiver and her teeth chatter. She clenched her jaw hard.

He stopped before her, closely inspecting her face. "What you need are some dry clothes and a brandy. You take care of the first, and I'll get you the second."

Figuring it was useless to argue and not really wanting to be alone just yet, anyway, Marissa opened a drawer in the chest and grabbed shorts and a T-shirt. Riley went directly to the kitchenette and the cabinet that held a shelf of miniature liquor bottles as if he was familiar with the place.

By the time she slipped into her clothes and quietly exited the bathroom a few minutes later, he was occupying one of the chairs in the sitting area, his back half-turned to her. Because of the angle, he didn't see her immediately, and Marissa took the opportunity to study him for a moment. Actually, this was the first time she'd seen Riley O'Hare in something other than moonlight.

To look at him, one would never have guessed he'd tangled with a poisonous snake mere minutes before. He was calm, his typical hard expression for once relaxed. What she could see of his face was sensually gripping—maybe too much so—for being attracted to a man whose ideals were so opposite her own could only mean trouble. Still, she couldn't help but admire his dark brown hair embellished with sun streaks. And she noticed that the green eyes he suddenly turned on her were almost identical to Luke's.

The difference was that the teenager was open, his emotions clearly laid out in his gaze and expression. His father could hardly claim the same.

Yet Marissa had no trouble reading Riley right now.

He was looking at her as if she were stark naked and he was liking the fact. His gaze held appreciation and a healthy lust that flustered her.

"Better?" he asked.

"Warmer."

Remembering that she had thrown her naked body against his made Marissa blush furiously and seek a distraction. A bulbous glass holding a generous splash of brandy waited for her on the rattan coffee table. She slid onto the couch and picked up the drink.

"To quick thinking," she muttered, wishing he would stop staring at her in that disturbing way— wishing part of her would stop liking it.

The brandy burned its way down into her stomach. She'd only taken a sip to test herself. A relaxing warmth quickly spread through her. Determined to take advantage of the feeling, she wedged herself in a corner against a bunch of brightly flowered pillows and pulled her legs up along the length of the couch.

"You're lucky you recognized a coral snake when you saw it," Riley said, his gaze once more inscrutable. "Ever seen one before?"

"In a zoo. Not quite the same thrill. Are they common around here?" Dreading the thought of another such experience, she shuddered.

"I've never heard of one being spotted on Lime Key before. Then again, snakes don't exactly go around with calling cards, announcing themselves."

"A fluke," she said, staring down into her glass. "And I had to find it." Just like Dori's body...

"Or it had to find you," Riley said.

Her head snapped up. "What does that mean?"

A stab of fear shot through Marissa not unlike the one she'd felt when she'd realized there was a snake on her foot. Her fingers tightened around the brandy glass, and she stared at the man whom she had fought with one minute and who had come to her rescue the next.

"Nothing," he finally said.

But staring at the restored facade that kept people out, Marissa wasn't so certain. Riley O'Hare's arrival had been timed perfectly. A more suspicious person might say he had been purposely providential.

If he knew about the snake...

But surely he wouldn't go to such measures—he wouldn't scare her half to death just to get her off the island. He hadn't had to approve her coming in the first place. Still, she couldn't help but be uneasy.

"What were you doing cruising my neighborhood, anyway?" She kept her tone light and followed the question with another sip of brandy.

"Taking a walk."

He was traversing the resort grounds after Ansel Roche had disclaimed any kind of friendly relationship between them? What had the resort owner said? Something about Riley O'Hare not liking poachers on his preserve. She would have thought the feeling would be reciprocal and that Riley would stay away from the resort for his part.

"So you were just taking a walk up to my front door?" she asked.

"I wanted to see you."

He was seeing her now and taking advantage again. His sultry gaze swept the length of her bare legs, making Marissa want to curl them up under her.

She stayed put. "Really."

"We got off on the wrong foot."

"Then this is an apology?"

He scowled. "Don't push it. I was going to suggest a truce."

"Why?"

"Because Kamiko doesn't need you to be stressed out." His response surprised her, though she didn't know why. After all, Riley was fully committed to helping dolphins living in captivity in any way he could.

"What is your background?"

"My background doesn't matter!" he snapped.

"I think it does. You're what? A trainer gone sour? A former curator at an aquarium? How do you know so much about dolphins?"

He seemed to relax a bit, as if he thought she'd been asking about something else and now realized his mistake. "The navy."

Even that fact he gave out reluctantly, and Marissa guessed why. "Marine mammal research."

For years, the navy had kept its work with marine mammals—dolphins, small whales and seals—under wraps, but now that the world was at peace of sorts, the military had declassified the information.

"I was an expert scuba diver when I enlisted at eighteen, so they sent me to Hawaii. I worked mostly with dolphins."

"Then you were a trainer just like I am," she said, unable to hold back her sense of triumph.

"Not hardly. I didn't teach them unnatural tricks to amuse an audience."

"No, you taught them far more deadly maneuvers."

Marine mammals had for some time been considered secret underwater weapons. Among other less barbarous examples, she'd read about experiments in Vietnam where dolphins had been taught to take a dart filled with carbon dioxide and puncture an enemy diver, causing him to explode.

"Actually, I worked on echolocation research."

Using echolocation—a natural form of sonar— dolphins and whales were able to "see" and to differentiate not only between shapes but also materials, such as various types of metals.

"And you're still doing that here."

He nodded.

"And you don't see that your using the dolphins isn't so very different from my working with them in an educational environment."

"Entertainment."

"Yes, we do entertain, as well as educate, at the oceanarium," Marissa admitted, her irritation with him growing. "People identify with the animals who perform for them, and they learn to be concerned for something larger in scope than their own lives." She took a deep breath. "If ordinary citizens had never had the chance to see and touch the wonderful creatures you and I both care about, the Marine Mammal Protection Act never would have been passed."

His laugh was biting. "The laws aren't sufficient and you know it."

"But it's a start. And things are getting better all the time. Our lobby is stronger. Tuna fishing—"

"It's getting late." As abruptly as he'd interrupted her, Riley rose. "I'll see to the remains of your, uh, visitor. And I'll let Roche know."

Somehow, that sounded like a threat.

Before Marissa could comment, he strode toward the door. Not another word. Not a backward glance. Then he was gone. His odd actions deflated her anger and left her puzzled. Par for the course. He never did or said what she expected, at least not for long.

She certainly hadn't expected to see him again this night. Shaking away the accompanying negative thought, she rose and locked her door, wondering if she should secure the windows, as well. The screens were protection against another dangerous visitor finding its way in.

As long as that visitor wasn't human...

ONCE MORE, RILEY didn't join them at breakfast the next morning, and Marissa experienced an odd sort of disappointment, though she would no doubt have been embarrassed had she been forced to face him with an audience. She wouldn't soon forget throwing her naked body against him. Nor would she forget about the snake. Pulse triggered the moment she'd opened her cabin door, she'd checked out the path carefully all the way to the refuge and would continue to do so.

She was thankful no one brought up the unfortunate incident. Riley obviously had kept his counsel. She couldn't help but wonder if he was avoiding her.

After breakfast she accompanied Vida to get "dolphin chow," as Erasmus called his catch. Located in a building with peeling paint between the dock and the pens was an ancient walk-in freezer that was also used for people food, no doubt because refuge workers took so many meals at the main house. The thick wooden door was heavy and awkward to keep open—Marissa figured the floor wasn't level and was gratified to see that the door had a safety handle on the inside.

Just in case...

Each dolphin had his or her own bucket. Vida lined them up on a stainless-steel counter and began filling them with fish for the morning feeding.

"That must have been spooky," she said, giving Marissa a sidelong glance. "Your finding Dori like you did."

Unprepared for the gruesome reminder, Marissa had trouble breathing normally. "More like she found me. And no, it wasn't pleasant."

"You could have drowned, too."

Marissa started at the matter-of-fact statement that was devoid of emotion or empathy. "But I didn't." And wondered at the woman's temerity.

"And you didn't see anyone else, right?"

As in the murderer? "Right." Would everyone at the refuge ask her about it?

Marissa stared at Vida, who seemed unconcerned. Her attention was studiously elsewhere as she referred to a chalk chart on a blackboard. Each dolphin was allotted an appropriate amount of rations according to its weight, and that amount was split into four meals to be distributed throughout the day. The largest of the dolphins—Brutus, the adult male—ate twenty-seven pounds of fish.

Vida was absorbed in her task as if she'd already forgotten her interest in Dori's death.

With only Kamiko to take care of, Marissa quickly filled her bucket, helped the blonde measure out the appropriate quotas for the others, then, believing in giving tit for tat, dared to broach what she figured was an equally sensitive subject for the other woman.

"You seem to know a lot about working with dolphins for someone who usually takes care of tourists and paperwork."

Vida's hesitation in dumping fish from the scale into a bucket was barely noticeable. "I was a part-time assistant trainer at a zoo while I was going to school." She straightened to her full six feet. "And Riley still holds it against me. Not that he would ever admit it. He always said the refuge didn't need another marine mammal specialist, and that I would have to wait my turn." Her tone grew bitter. "Then he lets a kid work with the dolphins as soon as he moves here."

"But Luke is Riley's son," Marissa said, disturbed by the woman's petulant tone. "He undoubtedly wants to train him, hoping that some day they'll run this place together."

"True." Vida's expression was still tense, but she almost sounded satisfied when she said, "Dori's gone for good now. He's going to have to replace her, and Luke's not going to fit the bill for a few more years."

Was that a really cold way of putting it, or was she reading malice where none was intended?

Remembering Vida's argument with Billie the morning before, Marissa said, "I take it you and Dori Lynch weren't the best of friends."

"Not by a long shot. Dori didn't have much use for people who couldn't do something for her...like other women. And she lucked out in getting everything she wanted. Or she just took it."

Marissa wondered if that was truth or jealousy speaking. Vida could appear friendly, but she had a biting tongue when it suited her. There was something two-faced about the blonde that made her uneasy. Before she could probe deeper, Luke banged through the door, Ken following.

"It's the three of us this morning," Ken said, gathering the handles of four loaded pails, two in each hand. "Riley's running some errands over on Key Largo."

So that's why he hadn't joined them for breakfast. It had nothing to do with her, thank goodness. Marissa was relieved. Feeling awkward around the man would be very uncomfortable. After all, she was going to be at the refuge for a week or two and couldn't exactly avoid Riley.

"If you need an extra hand, I'd be glad to help," Marissa told Ken. One person dealing with four adult dolphins for an entire day could be wearing.

"Thanks," Ken said as he headed toward the door. "I'll keep the offer in mind."

Luke took the three pails for the juvenile dolphins and followed Ken out of the building. Vida carried twin pails for Dreamer, the pregnant dolphin, and Shahar and Ali, the mother and her still-nursing calf, while Marissa had only Kamiko's breakfast to worry about.

Rather than just giving the fish to the dolphins, their caretakers made them work for their food a little at a time using various training or testing techniques. In this instance, Riley's attitude about not taking advantage of marine mammals wasn't applicable—in reality, the dolphins enjoyed the stimulation of working for their meals, as he well knew. It kept them from being bored.

The morning flew by and suddenly it was time for lunch.

Conspicuous by his absence, Riley was uppermost in her mind as she companionably shared the midday meal with the refuge workers. Every time she looked at Luke, she saw more of Riley in him ... and wondered about their relationship.

Not that anything but Kamiko was any of her business.

With that thought as a reminder, Marissa was the first one back out at the pens with a fresh bucket of fish and a couple of toys. Before she could resume her play with Kamiko, however, a powerfully built man stormed onto the main boardwalk from the direction opposite the house.

"Where the hell's O'Hare?" he boomed, glaring directly at her.

Marissa was so startled, she almost fell into the pen along with the ball she threw for Kamiko to chase. "Uh, he's not here right now." As far as she knew, he still hadn't returned from Key Largo.

The man's wiry, graying hair stood out all around his head as if punctuating his displeasure. "Then you're it!"

"It ... what?" She stood to face him.

"Come get your damned dolphin away from my property and back where he belongs before I shoot 'im!"

Her heart speeded up and she glanced over the pens. "One of the dolphins got out?"

"That's what I said, ain't it?"

Not exactly, but there was no point in arguing. She noted only three sleek bodies in the main pen. The fourth—and largest—was missing. Wondering how in the heck she was going to get a full-grown male dolphin she didn't even know back where he belonged, she was heartened when Vida made an appearance carrying two more buckets of fish.

"Thank goodness you're here." As Marissa watched the rude man stalk away, she quickly explained the problem.

"That's Toby Hanson," Vida told her. "He hates having the refuge next to his property, and he's tried to buy the land so he could close it down. He thinks it's an eyesore."

True, the place wasn't in prime condition, but it wasn't exactly a slum, either.

"He wants immediate action," Marissa said.

"I'll bet he does. Here, take this and let's get going." Vida shoved one of her buckets of fish at Marissa and started off at an easy jog.

The two women rushed over to the adjoining property. From Vida's sense of urgency, Marissa guessed Toby Hanson didn't like the individual dolphins any more than he did the idea of having a refuge next door to him. She only prayed he wouldn't do anything rash.

"Don't worry," Vida said, slowing a bit when they left the refuge property. "Brutus is a real sweetheart and a sucker for 'go get the fish.' We can probably lead him back using a trail of these little suckers," she added, indicating her bucket, "without ever having to get into the water with him."

Not that Marissa would have minded getting wet. "He's done this before?"

"Why do you think old Toby's ready to bust a gut?"

Marissa shook her head. She could understand someone being concerned that a dolphin had gotten out, but not angry that the animal was cruising his shoreline. "What did Brutus ever do to Toby?"

"He, uh, made advances on a woman who *used* to be Toby's girlfriend, if you know what I mean. The woman ran out of the water screaming and swearing she would never come back."

"Oops."

"Yeah, oops."

Seconds later, they came face-to-face with the man, who was still spitting mad.

"There he is." Toby Hanson pointed to the dorsal fin protruding from the blue-green water filling his small private bay. "Acting like he owns the place! Get him out of there. And see that he don't come back!"

He didn't even bother to wait around and see how they were going to accomplish this task, but rather stormed into his house, slamming the door behind him.

Fortunately, Vida's plan worked like a charm. The two women easily lured the dolphin back to the refuge by pretending this was all a game. A quarter of an hour later, Brutus was waiting outside his pen, whistling for entrance. Marissa slipped into the water with him, hands filled with fish that he greedily took from her.

When he rubbed himself against her provocatively, she took it good-naturedly, unlike Toby Hanson's ex-girlfriend. "Sorry, sport, wrong species," she said, laughing.

Luke came running, carrying some tools and a snorkeling mask. "Out again! Brutus, one of these days..." the teenager growled. He told Marissa, "He can get into open water all by himself, but for some reason, the big baby needs help getting back into his pen!"

The pen didn't seem imposing enough to keep any dolphin in or out, especially not at high tide. Marissa couldn't help remembering how Kamiko had vaulted a far higher barrier at the oceanarium. And why. She was grateful that Brutus had merely been having fun.

"Does he do this often?"

"Often enough," Vida said as Luke clambered into the water opposite Marissa and Brutus, who clicked and whistled. "Sometimes two or three times a week, although he doesn't always visit Hanson."

"I told Dad we should build an open-water gate into this pen," Luke added, "so we can just let Brutus back in after he takes his swim, but like everything else that needs to be done around here, it'll have to wait."

The three female dolphins whirled around him excitedly. Luke worked rapidly, unfastening part of the rusty fencing, slipping on his mask and going under for the rest. Marissa helped him roll the chain link back. The moment his path was free, Brutus shot inside, and he and his harem made an inspection tour of the entire pen while Luke resecured the rickety fencing.

Since Luke had brought it up, Marissa broached the topic of upkeep as she climbed out of the water. "Looks like you could do with new pens altogether."

"Yeah, that'd be great," the teenager said. "If only we had the money."

She looked over at Vida, since she was the one in charge of mailings. "Fund-raising isn't going well?"

"It would be a lot better if more people knew about the place." The blonde didn't attempt to hide her disgust at the situation. "We charge visitors for tours, but that's only once a day, three days a week, when it should be at least twice a day, six or seven days a week. But Riley refuses any chance for publicity."

So the owner's reclusiveness was the reason the refuge was in such shabby condition. Marissa figured she should have known. Of course he wouldn't want reporters trampling over his land any more than he liked having *her* there. But what a terrible waste. With proper public relations and publicity, he could get more people interested, thereby bringing in the money for needed repairs and improvements.

Considering how run-down the place was, she wondered how Riley could afford to support Luke when the boy was with his mother.

If he even did, that is.

Her own father had run a dive shop between treasure hunts, but nearly all the money from that venture had gone into his obsession. Her mother had been responsible for keeping a roof over their heads and food in their stomachs. Not that Mom had ever complained. Though Marissa had been resentful for her mother, she'd still worked summers at the shop with her father until the year he died. She couldn't help but compare the two men.

No sooner had she done so, than Riley himself appeared. Looking from Luke to Vida to her, he demanded, "What in the world is going on?"

"Brutus." Luke crossed his arms and gave his father a hostile look.

"He managed to get out into open water," Marissa said evenly, "but he's fine now."

Vida stood back and remained silent, her expression oddly smug.

Shaking his head in mock disgust, Riley eyed the dolphin, who now lingered near the humans wearing his best innocent expression. "What are we going to do with you, sport?"

His tone was light, but Marissa could feel the tension crackling between father and son.

"It's not *his* fault the pen isn't adequate to keep him in!" Luke snapped.

Riley calmly met his son's angry gaze. "So you're saying it's mine?"

Chilled by the cool tone he used with the teenager, Marissa had to force herself to stay out of it.

"You could do something about stuff around here if you wanted to," Luke was saying.

Marissa figured Riley probably would if he could.

"The money coming in from tourists and donations is barely enough to keep this place going," he said. "But if we get that grant from Ocean Watch that I applied for—"

"Who cares about some dumb grant?" Luke countered. "You won't know about it for months, anyhow."

"Part of growing up is learning to be patient."

"Learning to be? I've been patient all my life!" Suddenly Luke was yelling. "If Mom hadn't forced you to take me—"

"Your mother didn't force me to do anything I didn't want to do."

But Luke wasn't buying any of it. "You could get the money if you really wanted to, but you won't ever be able to hack the family stuff!" With that, the teenager whirled and fled.

"Luke!" His expression now as grim as she'd ever seen it, Riley stormed after his son. "Luke, come back here!"

Marissa let go of the breath she hadn't realized she'd been holding. Though he might have a heart for animals, Riley O'Hare came up short when people were involved. Especially with the ones close to him. Not that she should be concerned. What he did was none of her business, after all. She had no relationship with Riley. Nor did she want one.

She would only be at Dolphin Haven for a few more days. A week, tops.

Then she would probably never see Riley O'Hare again.

SHE WAS STILL ALIVE. The Gilmore woman had more going for her than met the eye.

How many women would have recognized a coral snake?

How many would have kept their heads, acting rationally rather than panicking?

Impressive.

And frustrating.

She was a worthy adversary... even if she didn't realize she was a target. Killing her outright would be too easy. And dangerous. Then the authorities would look closer to home for the murderer. As it was, that fool of a detective in charge of the case believed drug runners had been after the boat.

Why spoil the illusion?

Surely there were myriad other ways to make murder look like an accident.

Chapter Four

"Doris Lynch's death was no accident."

Dressed in chinos, an open-necked flowered shirt and sneakers, Detective Nick Lujan paced the length of the deck as he made the pronouncement. Riley's eyebrows shot up. His discussion of Kamiko's progress with Marissa had been interrupted for this? He didn't need another annoyance after his son's earlier outburst. He was barely a degree away from exploding.

"Tell me something we don't already know," he demanded.

"What I meant was, she wasn't accidentally *murdered*."

In the seat across from him, Marissa shifted restlessly and plucked at the single braid spilling over her shoulder. "But your theory about the drug runners—"

"Only a theory. Doesn't hold water."

"So you've found other evidence?" Riley asked, suddenly tense.

From the corner of his eye, he saw Billie standing behind the kitchen screen, staring. He'd asked her to bring them some ice tea and she had a full tray in her hands. So what was she waiting for?

"I just came back from Key West where I talked to Doris Lynch's mother," Lujan was saying.

"And?"

"Seems Mrs. Lynch thinks her daughter got herself killed over some big secret." The cop stopped in front of Riley, his near-black eyes boring into him, pinning him where he sat. "You got any secrets, Mr. O'Hare?"

Stomach immediately knotting, Riley steeled himself to show no reaction. "None worth killing over."

"Mrs. Lynch was pretty specific. She said the secret had to do with the refuge."

Purposely leaning back against the railing as if his whole life were open to inspection—which, of course, it wasn't—Riley waved a hand. "I'm all ears." How many people had Dori told?

"She didn't know what it was exactly."

His stomach relaxed. "And you call that 'pretty specific'? Look, Detective Lujan, the poor woman is still in shock over her daughter's death. Her grief is doing the talking. She wants someone to blame."

"You."

"Figured that. Only problem is, I didn't do it."

Lujan leaned in closer. A lock of his blue-black hair fell over one eyebrow, giving him a menacing look...as if he had an intimate acquaintance with the streets...as if that acquaintance had been on the opposite side of the law. "Then who did?"

"If I knew, I'd—"

"What?" Lujan interrupted. "Kill him?"

Features twisting into a scowl, Riley baited the cop. "Make sure he got the justice he deserves."

"Are you capable of murder, Mr. O'Hare?"

Riley heard the screen door creak open and noted Billie's approach into his peripheral vision.

"How do you know it was a man?"

Marissa's question startled them both and made Billie lose a beat on the steps. She wavered and the tray swayed. Riley was certain the pitcher was a goner, but the housekeeper saved herself and the tea.

Riley asked Marissa, "You think a woman did it?"

At the same time, Lujan prompted, "You remembered something."

"No, nothing," Marissa told the cop. Her clear blue gaze turned to Riley. "I think a woman is capable of murder."

This woman was capable of doing just about anything—Riley was sure of it—but he doubted Marissa Gilmore could take another person's life even to save her own. She was tough on the outside, able to handle animals many times her own weight. Able to handle him. But there was a softness in her that he sensed more than saw. He'd had a glimpse of it when she'd thrown herself into his arms, at first heedless of her own nudity, then embarrassed by it. He'd wanted to take that softness and—

But getting caught up in some fantasy wouldn't help him here. With Detective Nick Lujan playing a cat-and-mouse game with him, he couldn't afford to be distracted.

"Dori was fit and strong because of her work here at the refuge," he said. "The murderer would have had to be even stronger."

"Or would have had to surprise her." Marissa turned to Lujan. "How much strength does it take to cut off someone's air long enough to knock them out?"

"Not as much as you might think." The cop waited until Billie set down the tray and was filling glasses before saying, "Now back to that secret. Got any idea what Doris Lynch meant?"

"Maybe it was just her overactive imagination," Riley offered.

Billie backed him up. "Dori was always a fanciful young woman." She handed the detective an overly full glass and tea splashed his flowered shirt.

Swiping at it with a large hand, Lujan asked, "How so?"

"Dori thought she could have anything she wanted," the housekeeper said. "Work related or personal."

Lujan flashed Riley a significant look. Let him look all he wanted. The cop wasn't getting any secrets out of him.

"So you're saying she was spoiled? Selfish?"

"She didn't exactly flaunt it," Billie answered, filling the remaining glass, "but, yeah, Dori was both of those."

"Give me an example."

Taking one of the drinks, Riley met Billie's panic-stricken gaze and immediately covered for the housekeeper. "Dori insisted on having days off when it suited her even if it meant walking off the job." The truth. Especially during the last month or so.

Riley remembered her last excuse—a doctor's appointment—and wondered if that's when she'd learned of her pregnancy.

"Days off? That's it?" Lujan sounded incredulous.

"You asked for an example," Riley said, sensing Marissa's uneasiness with his explanation. "I gave you one."

"I asked your housekeeper for an example."

Billie set a glass of ice tea in front of Marissa, distracting the other woman for the moment. "I don't like speaking ill of the dead."

"Uh-huh. What about of the living?"

Lujan was staring at him again, and Riley didn't like it. "If you've got something biting you, let's have it."

"No accusations. Yet. Just lotsa questions." The cop took a long swig of the ice tea. "Questions make me thirsty, and I got lots more for your employees. And the other residents of Lime Key." Another swallow. "You don't object to my asking around about this supposed secret, do you?"

A trickle of sweat worked its way down Riley's spine. "No. No objections at all," he lied.

What if Lujan learned the truth?

Having learned long ago to keep his hand close to his chest, Riley forced himself to look at least somewhat relaxed. He would deal with the situation when it came up. *If* it came up. Apart from Cole Glaser, Billie was the only other one who knew, and his housekeeper was loyal.

She would do anything to keep his secret safe.

SECRETS. Did Riley O'Hare have a few or was she merely imagining things? Marissa wondered. Throughout the rest of the afternoon—probably because the detective was still somewhere around the key asking questions—she couldn't get her mind off the odd conversation between the two men. They'd baited each other as if they were truly on opposing sides.

Riley was hiding something and Lujan knew it.

But what?

Keeping something private didn't mean a person was a murderer, she assured herself. While growing up, she'd kept the knowledge of her father's fixation on finding sunken treasure to herself for fear that her friends would laugh at him. And her. Not that his preoccupation had anything to do with a death.

Done with Kamiko for the day, Marissa headed for her temporary home, once more using the back path. The afternoon was blazing hot and the humidity so high it should be raining, facts that could be ignored while working in or near water. But being in the midst of a subtropical atmosphere intensified her discomfort, and the thick, junglelike undergrowth reminded her of the snake. Her eyes quickly scanned the path ahead. All clear.

She'd gotten about halfway there when she heard voices, hushed but angry.

"Don't even think about it!"

Riley. Drawn by the urgency in his tone, Marissa changed direction to find out what was going on.

"You don't tell me what to do."

A second voice—familiar—though she couldn't quite identify it.

"Don't get too smug."

"Out of my way!"

The sound of a struggle lent speed to Marissa's feet and she rounded one of the cabins in time to see two men tussling in the thick vegetation. Riley O'Hare was strong-arming Cole Glaser into submission. When Glaser made a valiant attempt to wrench himself free of the stranglehold, Riley grabbed him by the neck and threw him up against a coconut tree, bracing him there so that his feet were practically off the ground.

"I'm not screwing around, Glaser, and you'd better not, either . . . or else."

Marissa's stomach clenched at the intimation of further violence. What in the world was going on? She'd had no idea the two men had ever met. As far as she knew, Cole Glaser was merely a guest at the resort.

"Okay, okay, you made your point," the sandy-haired man finally rasped.

Riley let go of him so suddenly the smaller man crashed to the ground and sprawled amongst the low-growing ferns. A skittering noise indicated some small animal's frantic retreat. Equally quick, Glaser got to his feet and sped away in the general direction of the restaurant-bar, crashing noisily through the undergrowth.

Marissa tried to back off silently. Unnoticed. But, as if instinct alerted him to her presence, Riley turned and speared her with his gaze. Heart pounding, pulse racing, she froze. She had no idea of what she'd stumbled onto, but from his expression, Riley was as furious with her as he'd been with Glaser.

"What the hell are you doing here?" he demanded. "Why didn't you say something?"

Unwilling to show any fear, she said, "Tit for tat. You don't announce yourself—"

"Quit the wisecracks."

He was stalking her, making her insides quiver. Making it nearly impossible for her to stand there—seemingly calm—and face him down. His anger was a tangible thing. When he stood so close that he lit her nerve endings, she had to fight the temptation to run as Glaser had. As if her shaky knees would hold her for more than a step or two, anyway....

"Get an earful?" he asked.

Boldly she admitted, "Only half. Want to tell me what's going on?"

Expression threatening, he moved into her space, stripping her of any comfort zone. "What's going on is that I don't like people prying into my business."

"Is that what Cole Glaser was doing?"

"You know him?"

"He's staying at the resort," Marissa reminded him. "Considering it's the only place on the island to get dinner, it would be hard to miss him."

Riley's expression lightened. Slightly. Not that Marissa relaxed any. His mere presence made her tense, even when he was in a friendlier mood. Change that to polite. She wasn't certain he was ever friendly. A woman would have to put up with a lot to have a relationship with a man like him.

Realizing where her thoughts were leading her— aghast that the sexual attraction hadn't cooled after several unsatisfying encounters with the man—Marissa probed, "So what were you arguing about?" She'd always been one to test fate, but she'd rather have him feel irritated than anything else right now. "What made you so angry you looked ready to kill the man?"

Her exaggeration got to Riley. The scowl deepened and he narrowed the gap between their faces so that his warm breath fanned her skin. Despite herself, she felt her pulse speed up.

"You're only here with my reluctant permission," he reminded her. "Unless you want to take your fanny back to where you belong, stay the hell out of my business!''

Her mouth fell open, and though she dearly wished she could come back with something equally caustic, not a word followed as he stormed off toward the refuge. She stood there staring. Considering. Riley had a point—his connection with Cole Glaser really was none of her business. So why had she felt the need to poke her nose where it didn't belong? Why did she want to know more about the enigmatic owner of Dolphin Haven than he was willing to share?

Continuing on toward her cabin, Marissa suddenly felt as if she'd been struck by a thunderbolt. Despite his reputation…despite their differences…despite the fact that he was far from being easy to know…Riley O'Hare was exactly the sort of man who could get under her defenses.

No, not *sort of,* but *the* man.

Far from being a masochist, Marissa was appalled at herself. Riley's obsession was apparently more important to him than people, as demonstrated by his relationships with his son and Dori, undoubtedly the mother of his unborn child. Her own bond with her father had been frustrating enough. She didn't need to open herself to another man with a fixation.

And if she was reading Detective Nick Lujan right, Riley O'Hare was a prime suspect.

Finally hitting home, the idea of harboring a killer in their midst—possibly someone from the refuge itself—sent a frisson of fear down her spine. Even though she'd been the one to find Dori's body, the actual murder had held a certain remoteness when she'd believed some nameless drug runner had been responsible.

But that, obviously, hadn't been the case. And she was unlucky enough to be stuck here until Kamiko was totally settled in.

When she reached her cabin, Marissa couldn't get inside fast enough. Her hands shook as she bolted the door. Then she realized her foolishness. No reason for *her* to be apprehensive. Whatever the murderer's motives—whatever this secret was that Mrs. Lynch insisted on—they had nothing to do with her. As an outsider, she was safe as long as she kept to herself and concentrated on her job. Not an easy task with a distraction like Riley O'Hare around.

Dear God, what if she was attracted to the murderer himself?

"I'm so glad you accepted my invitation," Ansel Roche said as they sped across Florida Bay toward Key Largo later that evening.

"I never would have thought such a beautiful island could cause me to feel so claustrophobic." Marissa had to raise her voice over the roar of the speedboat's motor and the noisy crash of waves. "An excursion was exactly what I needed."

Especially if she wanted to get her mind off more serious issues, not to mention Riley O'Hare and his threats. To be honest, anger both with him and with herself had prompted her to take Ansel up on his offer to get her off the island for a few hours.

"You looked like you could use a friend. You hardly touched your dinner."

If Ansel expected an explanation, Marissa didn't give him more than a smile. She wasn't about to involve the owner of Lime Tree Resort in the refuge's troubles. It wasn't her place to do so, anyway.

Besides, she didn't want to put words to her unfounded fears. That might make them more tangible.

Cutting the motor as they entered a canal, he let the craft drift toward a harbor area and nosed it into a vacant slip, explaining that he rented it on an ongoing basis. He also kept a spot in the adjoining lot for his car, a white Le Baron convertible.

"I love living on Lime Key." Ansel punched in eight-five-four-seven on the security pad that unlocked the car, then escorted Marissa around to the passenger side and opened the door for her. "But I'm not one to be confined on a tiny island. Having the freedom to come and go as I please gives me the best of both worlds. Often, a needed breather."

"I can appreciate the concept."

She'd hardly taken an easy breath since her encounter with Riley. But, sinking back into the luxurious car as Ansel started the engine, she felt infinitely better. She was neither a prisoner on that island, nor had she anything to fear. And this spur-of-the-moment outing with a handsome and sophisticated escort, who didn't threaten her every time she turned around, would do wonders for her psyche.

He drove a few miles before turning off on a side road leading toward the Atlantic. They pulled up to Largo Lights, a night spot connected to a sprawling resort crawling with people despite it being the off-season.

"Quite a difference from Lime Tree Resort," Marissa said as they crossed the parking lot to the entrance, where a group of young people in their early to midtwenties stood talking and laughing.

"Yes, isn't it? For one, it's a money-maker."

"Your place may be small, but I'll bet it's popular during the tourist season."

From the classy way he dressed, not to mention his fancy boat and car, Ansel didn't seem to be doing too badly for himself.

"I have a waiting list every weekend other than the summer months," he admitted. "Some weeks, too, especially around the holidays. It's frustrating that I can't do anything about losing all that business."

"You could easily double the number of cabins, though it would spoil the feeling of semi-isolation."

"Exactly. That's what makes Lime Tree Resort so special."

Cupping her elbow, he escorted her inside. Largo Lights was dark and smoky and noisy. Tiny Italian lights strung along the ceiling gave the appearance of stars. Candles at the tables and hanging lanterns at the large bar, near the rest rooms and alongside the double doors leading to an outside deck were the only other sources of illumination other than the stage lights. A band played country rock so loudly Marissa figured they'd only be able to talk during intermission. The dance floor was crowded with gyrating bodies.

Ansel ducked his head to say something to the hostess, who promptly led them through the crowd to the outside deck where the raucous sounds receded somewhat. Only a few other couples occupied the area, so they had their choice of tables, settling on one in a corner with some privacy.

With her permission, Ansel ordered two kirs. Marissa relaxed, spread out the skirt of her backless sundress, and turned her face up to the breeze sweeping the deck and carrying the scent of nearby orchids. A full moon settled in a sky that was dusted with stars and powder-puffed with clouds.

Such a romantic setting . . .

Such a waste . . !

"It's a lovely night, and this is a perfect place to enjoy it," Marissa told Ansel. He was gorgeous. Perfect. Too bad he failed to stir her hormones. "Though you don't seem like the country-rock type."

Indeed, though he wore a casual pastel flowered shirt and pale yellow trousers, he seemed far more sophisticated than the other men in the crowd, most of whom wore loud shorts and louder T-shirts.

"It's close by and the music selection varies, depending on the night. Key West is the place to go for the real Florida Keys nightlife . . . though it's faster to get to Miami."

"True, especially by car."

The overseas highway to Key West was notoriously jammed with traffic, especially during rush hours or on weekends. The hundred-mile drive could easily take the better part of four hours.

"So do you come up to the Miami area often?" she asked.

His expression shifted slightly. Deepened. As if he were trying to look inside her. "Often enough. When it suits my purposes."

Thinking he'd gotten the wrong idea—that she was interested because she herself lived in that area—Marissa was glad when Ansel changed the subject, asking about her interest in marine mammals. She'd hardly gotten started when their drinks arrived.

They toasted, "To new friends," and took a sip.

"So how do you like Dolphin Haven?" he asked, setting down his glass.

Conflicting emotions warred within Marissa, but she kept an even smile while saying, "It's an interesting place."

"With interesting people?"

"Some."

"I hope you don't make the same mistake that Dori Lynch made."

Her smile dimmed and her heart skipped a beat. "You mean getting myself killed?"

"I mean getting involved with Riley O'Hare."

Her breath caught in her throat for a moment. Was it so apparent? How could he know? Unless he'd overheard one of their arguments and had been savvy enough to read through the hostility and sense her attraction.

"I don't intend to do any such thing," she told him truthfully. "The master of Dolphin Haven and I don't exactly get along."

Ansel was sitting back, swishing the kir in its stemmed glass, his gaze intent on her face once more. "He has a way with women. He seduces them. Then breaks their hearts."

With his tanned, golden good looks, Ansel himself could easily be a heartbreaker. And yet he was easier to get along with than Riley—the kind of man she *should* be attracted to. Only she wasn't. Spending time with him was merely a pleasant diversion.

"You mean Dori," she finally said.

"She was his last victim, yes."

Victim. As in murder? Surely not. Surely he was only talking about a crime of the heart.

"You knew her well?"

"Not really, until after...she needed someone to talk to who wasn't connected to the refuge." Ansel's manner sobered. "I was available and willing. I liked Dori. She was a good person. She didn't deserve to be murdered. Not that anyone does," he hastily added.

His good opinion of Dori was refreshing to hear, but she wondered if he was alone in that. Billie and Vida certainly hadn't had anything positive to say about the dead woman. And Riley had broken off with her.

"So you got to know Dori pretty well?"

He took a sip of his drink and nodded. "I spent some quality hand-holding time with Dori after Riley rejected her so cruelly. She never said so, exactly—I mean, Dori wouldn't, she was too good-hearted a person—but I suspect it had more to do with the pregnancy than anything."

Marissa started. First of all, this didn't sound like the Dori she'd been hearing about. Second, she'd figured Riley hadn't known about the baby. But if he *had* known and had then kissed Dori off... that would be unconscionable. Though she'd been thinking along similar lines when it came to Riley and responsibility, Marissa didn't want to believe he could be *that* callous.

"Dori was only a couple of months along," Marissa mused. Or else the pregnancy wouldn't have been such a surprise, she reasoned silently. "Didn't she and Riley break up quite a while ago? If so, then he couldn't have known." Or was she reaching?

"Yes, well, perhaps you are correct," Ansel said, his tone neutral. "I hope I haven't offended you."

"No. Why would you think that?"

"You merely sound... so defensive of a man who doesn't deserve your loyalty."

Yet another dig at Riley. She wondered what lay between the two men. Dori?

Picking up her glass, she gave him another of her not-too-bright smiles. "Would you mind if we changed the subject?"

"Certainly."

Ansel was smooth. She would give him that. Or sensitive. Why not sensitive? Why did she have this feeling that everything he said and did was studied—as if for effect? He might well be trying to enlist her sympathies against Riley. But why? Had that been the plan for the evening?

Put off balance by the thought, Marissa could no longer relax in the man's company, and so, when she finished her kir and he suggested they have another, she demurred.

"I hope you don't mind going back, but it's been a long day. I'm afraid I overestimated my capacity for staying out late. I still have to see to Kamiko before I get to bed."

"She's not doing well?"

"Off her feed a little. I thought I would try to get her interested in her chow one more time before giving up for the night."

Calling the waitress over, Ansel immediately settled the bill. They were on their way back to the dock within minutes. He was quiet, introspective, as if—after planting the seeds of doubt about Riley—he really had nothing more to say to her. Or was her imagination working overtime?

She thought it might be, when halfway across the watery expanse to Lime Key, Ansel said, "I hope you'll come out with me again sometime soon."

Reluctant to agree, she said vaguely, "It would have to be soon. I'll only be here another week."

He looked at her intently. "So little time."

Marissa supposed she should be flattered, but for some reason, she wasn't. And the lack of chemistry had little to do with the odd sense of unease she was now feeling. It had something to do with Riley, she was certain. Were they rivals? Did Ansel see her as some kind of chess piece?

Back at the Lime Tree Resort dock, she allowed Ansel's swift kiss on her cheek only because it was easier than ducking him and perhaps creating a scene. Sensing someone was watching them intently, she looked over his shoulder toward the restaurant. Staring through the screened wall from the bar area was Cole Glaser. Though she recognized him, she couldn't see his face—couldn't tell what he thought of her being with the owner of the resort—but he continued to stare, making no secret of his interest.

"Thanks again for the drink," she said, but Ansel was already turning away.

With a last glance over at Glaser, who persisted in staring at her as he raised a beer bottle to his lips, Marissa walked toward the refuge. Unless she headed for her cabin first and then took the back path, she would have to pass the house and chance Riley's seeing her. Refusing to go out of her way, she instead moved as stealthily as possible. She'd rounded the house and was on the path to the shed holding the dolphin food, when she heard a scraping noise from the deck area.

Thinking she was caught in the act yet again, she stopped and turned; no glowering, dark-haired man came up from behind to give her a piece of his mind.

Another noise. A footfall as furtive as her own. Staring into the blackness surrounding the back of the house, she saw movement—a dark, stooped form under the deck. A man. Large and stocky. Toby Hanson? No, Toby was more solid and powerful rather than merely stocky. This looked more like Erasmus North! But what in the world would he be doing here at night, never mind sneaking around?

As quickly as she questioned the fisherman's presence, the figure was gone...almost as if she'd imagined it.

Marissa thought to call out, but if it had been Erasmus and he hadn't wanted his presence known, he certainly wouldn't have answered. Her challenge would only serve to alert anyone in the house. Like Riley. No doubt the man's appearance had some simple explanation, anyway. Perhaps something had dropped from his pocket that morning when he'd had his coffee on the deck, and he'd just now come back to look for the lost object.

Uneasy, but willing to accept a simple explanation—she didn't need to get further entangled in the affairs of the refuge—Marissa continued on to the building housing the dolphin kitchen. Since it was unlocked, she had no difficulty entering. Turning on a light, she went straight for the freezer and wrested open the heavy wooden door.

The cold air hit her hard, making her heated skin, which was damp with humidity, crawl with gooseflesh. Realizing she needed something to hold the fish, she rubbed her arms and backtracked, fetching the bucket marked with a *K* for Kamiko. The door had inched closed, and Marissa made certain she opened it wider before entering the double-chambered freezer that was the size of two small side-by-side closets. The outer room was well stocked with people food, while shelves in the inner room held nothing but dolphin chow.

Wishing she had brought a flashlight—the freezer light being out of commission was yet another item to add to the growing refuge fix-it list—Marissa paused a moment while her eyes adjusted. Enough light shone from the food-preparation room for her to see several pans of frozen fish. Her breath clouded around her mouth as she moved from the outer chamber to the inner.

And behind her, the door hinges creaked.

Startled, she stopped and glanced over her shoulder. The thick wooden panel was swinging inward ever so slightly... and then it stopped with a couple of feet to spare.

She let out a breath and went for the dolphin food. The fish were frozen together, so she set down her bucket and tried to break individual pieces off, a more difficult task than she'd imagined. She tried pounding a frozen sheet on a shelf edge, but that did nothing but make the room vibrate. She was going to need something sharp to manage it. A knife or other tool. Barely familiar with the food-preparation area, she only hoped she would be able to find something appropriate.

As she turned to start her search, the door creaked again. Creaked and slowly swung inward. She flew toward the narrowing light, but she slipped on something icy beneath one foot. Catching herself and regaining her balance took precious seconds. She rushed to keep the door from closing altogether.

Too late.

The click echoed throughout the dark space, and for a moment, Marissa stood as frozen as the fish she'd come to get for Kamiko.

Her heart raced. But no need to panic, she told herself. The door had an inside handle. A safety release. She would get out, and before coming back inside for the fish, she would find something heavy to hold the door open.

Enveloped in absolute darkness, she felt her way along the icy wall, back to the door and the blessed safety release, a metal bar with a wooden grip. But when she tried to lift it, the thing didn't budge.

Was it stuck, or was there merely a trick to opening the damn door?

"Don't panic," she told herself, saying the words aloud to make herself feel better. "You'll get out of here. Stay calm and try again."

But a second try was no more successful than the first. The handle refused to yield. She tried lifting. Pushing. Pulling. Turning. Nothing worked.

With a squeal of frustration, she jerked the thing as hard as she could.

It was moving!

But Marissa's elation was short-lived as the wood-covered piece of metal came free in her hand.

Chapter Five

"Damn piece of junk!" Marissa cried in frustration, hands gripping the broken lever so tightly that the metal nearly cut through her flesh.

The realization that she was well and truly stuck hit her hard. As did the fact that she was cold. And getting colder. And she'd only been inside the freezer for a few minutes, exerting energy at that. She couldn't stay here much longer. Not if she was going to survive.

What to do?

Was she doomed to freeze to death?

"Help!" she yelled, feeling foolish even as the word left her mouth.

Who would hear her? The freezer's walls were as thick as the door, not to mention well insulated. No one would come for her. Her knees nearly gave way as Marissa realized she had to figure a way out herself. Terrific. Stuck in the dark with nothing but the faulty door handle, how was she supposed to manage it?

"Don't panic. Don't panic."

But she *was* panicking. Her stomach took a tumble and her pulse raced through her so quickly, its rush blocked out all other noises . . . as if she could hear anything outside of this well-padded dungeon.

She took deep breaths. Lots of them. Finally her stomach settled down and her pulse steadied a bit. She was running on pure adrenaline now.

"Think!"

Marissa ran her hands over the wooden panel and around its perimeter, hoping to find some fault, some fingerhold she could use as leverage to pry herself out of there. Nothing. Of course the one thing that would be solid in this steadily crumbling place would be the very door holding her prisoner!

She screamed in frustration. She screamed in rage. She screamed on general principles. She screamed until she had no breath left. Her adrenaline was pumping like crazy and venting her emotions made her feel better. Stronger. She would not sit back and wait to die.

She would think; she would figure a way out.

A semicalm minute later, it came to her. She'd have to use the only tool available—the ragged end of the broken safety release—to break a hole through the wooden door. She felt around the panel and chose her spot carefully. The area surrounding the hole where the release handle had been should be the weakest. Over and over she slashed at the solid wood. It crunched under her fierce onslaught. Chips flew. She stopped every few strokes and felt the damage. The going was extremely slow, but she had no alternative.

It didn't take long for her arm to react to the effects of the blows. Her strokes became weaker. Frustration made her take the tool with both hands and put all her strength behind her next attack. More splintering wood. Elated, she moved to draw back the bar to try again…but it wouldn't yield. The metal bar was stuck well and good. She shifted position to get better leverage, but still couldn't budge the thing.

Closing her eyes, Marissa let her forehead drop against the door. She'd done this to herself. She'd sneaked out to feed Kamiko at night, despite Riley's warning not to wander around by herself. She'd known the door was apt to swing shut on its own, yet she hadn't secured it. This was all her fault. No one else to blame.

A frustrated Marissa gave the makeshift tool another tug. When it refused to give, she started banging on the door again and again with both fists.

"Damn! Damn! Damn!"

The shriek of metal shot through her curses and suddenly the door swung open. Light seared her eyes, making her blink and avoid it for a second. Then she focused.

The vision before her was becoming all too familiar.

Scowling and shaking his head, Riley stood there, his gaze driving into her. "Who did you inherit your good sense from, anyhow?"

"I—if you would f-fix things around here…" She was shaking too hard from the cold and the fright to finish. This time it was no accident. This time she threw herself against him on purpose. "Oh, that's better," she murmured, burrowing into his warmth.

In all likelihood confounded by her action, he stood stiffly for a second before wrapping both arms around her. "You could have frozen to death."

"Tell me something I don't know."

She shivered against him and he swept both hands slowly along her back, left naked by the stylish sundress. She was grateful for anything that could make her feel warm again. Then heat began coursing through her. Not only the comfort of flesh touching flesh, but a heat that went deeper, all the way to her core. Riley's touch turned her from a woman who sought warmth and reassurance into one with more basic needs begging to be taken care of.

Embarrassed at being so easily seduced by Riley's touch, Marissa struggled out of his arms. "Thanks, I'm feeling better now. No snakes for you to kill tonight."

He didn't respond to her humor. His expression was thoughtful ... and a bit grim. Catching sight of the broken safety release jutting out of the splintered wood, he grabbed hold of it.

Of course it came free in his hand. Easily.

"I couldn't figure out what I was hearing," he said. "Good thing you were so desperate, or I might have turned off the light in here and gone back to the house."

It was then that she realized he was wearing nothing more than a bathing suit, a towel and a spattering of salt water that hadn't yet dried. He'd been coming from the dolphin pens.

"Good thing," she echoed softly, averting her eyes from the torso that had to be the model of male perfection.

"Are you sure you're all right? You don't need a doctor?"

"I'm fine. No doctor. I might have a few sore muscles in the morning, though," she joked, rubbing her arms.

Marissa couldn't fathom what Riley might be thinking. His expression was almost...inviting. Then, before her very eyes, it subtly changed.

"So are you going to tell me what you were doing in here or do I have to play twenty questions?"

Marissa sighed and instructed her hormones to behave. "Kamiko was off her feed."

"And you were going to make up for it now with a late night snack."

"Instead, I made a mess of things."

"And almost got yourself killed in the process."

Killed. As in murdered? A chill that had nothing to do with the freezer swept through her. Surely he couldn't mean that!

She looked away from him to the door she'd half destroyed. "If you give me the name of a repair service, I'll be glad to have the damage taken care of."

"Not necessary."

"I know things around here are tight—"

"Forget it," he insisted, his tone brooking no argument. "So where's the fish for Kamiko?"

"Where I found it." She eyed the maw of the offending chamber. "Uh, she still needs to eat."

He fetched the fish for her. She couldn't go back into that freezer, not even with the door propped open, not even with Riley there. Again.

Odd how her life had been jeopardized two nights in a row and he'd been quick to her rescue both times. And both times they'd had arguments earlier....

A coincidence. Had to be.

"Here we go," Riley said, reentering the food-preparation area. He swung the bucket in one hand and closed the freezer door with the other.

She tried to take the dolphin chow from him, but he wouldn't give it over. "I can do this for you."

"Kamiko is my responsibility." Before he had a chance to object, she added, "I take my responsibilities seriously."

"Okay, then we'll go see her together. I'm not letting you out of my sight. Yet."

Fortunately, her hormones had decided to behave for the moment, and Riley acted as if nothing had happened between them. They strolled toward the pens in a near comfortable silence, only her awareness of him making her a little edgy.

Also fortunately, Kamiko decided she was willing to make up for the food she'd missed earlier. Within minutes of arriving at the pens, the fish were history, and Marissa was ready to head for her quarters where she could fall back on her bed and let go. Her adrenaline was finally running down, and she felt as if she'd gone through the mill.

"Why don't you come up to the house with me for a while," Riley suggested when she started to leave. "I could use some company."

She doubted it. He seemed like a man who did fine on his lonesome. Marissa figured Riley made the suggestion for her sake and wondered if she should be suspicious of his newly solicitous manner.

"You don't have to do that. I'll be fine."

"I never do anything I don't want to do."

If truth be known, she wasn't crazy about the idea of being alone just yet. Back in Miami, she led a quiet life compared to her first couple of days at the refuge. She'd never had a serious brush with death before. Marissa shook herself. She was getting a tad melodramatic here. Maybe she ought to be grateful for the offer.

"Sure," she finally said, "I wouldn't mind some company myself."

Even if that company was a man about whom she had very mixed feelings.

Which made her wonder how Riley felt about her....

She was still wondering when he led her into the house, dark but for a night-light in the kitchen. He hit a switch and the room was illuminated. Contrary to the exterior of the house, the kitchen was in good condition and fairly up-to-date.

"I don't know why, but I expected to see Billie here. She seems to be a permanent fixture in your kitchen."

"I'm not a slave driver," he protested. "Billie's actually free to do whatever she wants after lunch cleanup. She always insists on making dinner for me, though. Now for me and Luke," he amended.

"Where is your son?"

"Probably downstairs in the dark, listening to that hip-hop stuff."

Not hearing any irritating sounds issuing from below, she raised her eyebrows. "If he was, I think we'd know."

"Not necessarily. I bought him headphones first thing when he moved in. He and Billie each have a couple of rooms on the ground level, and his preference in noise would have driven her away for sure."

"I doubt that. She seems too loyal. *She* probably would have bought the headphones if you hadn't thought of it first."

Riley grinned, the startling expression softening his hard face. "You're probably right. Billie and I have an unusual relationship. I pay her salary, but she treats me more like a son than a boss."

"And that's okay with you?"

"Shouldn't it be?"

A mother-son relationship indicated a certain closeness she couldn't fathom him welcoming. Not that she was about to spoil their momentary truce by saying so.

So she said, "I think it sounds nice." Which she did. "We can all use someone to look after us sometimes." She wondered about his real parents...if they were still alive.

Suddenly Marissa realized that, for all intents and purposes, they were alone. She didn't know why the idea titillated her—they'd been alone before, after all. Maybe it was Riley's state of undress. A light matting of dark hair along his chest and stomach disappeared into his brief bathing suit. Realizing she was inspecting him a bit too closely—and aware that he knew it—she flushed and fought to think of some innocuous comment that would get her off the hook.

Riley did it for her. "Why don't you wait in here while I change," he said, indicating the next room.

He turned his back on her and continued through the doorway, so she didn't have a chance to gauge his reaction.

Following at a distance, Marissa wandered into the comfortably furnished combination dining and living room—a huge, open, high-ceilinged space that took up the center third of the upper floor. The room was simply furnished with tan and gray couches and chairs, and the wall-to-wall carpeting was a practical combination of the muted colors. Driftwood and shells and photographs of wildlife, including marine mammals, added touches of interest in an otherwise bland room.

Riley disappeared through a doorway to the left, closing the door behind him. Another doorway to the right remained open, revealing a bathroom and an office. As in similar Florida houses she'd visited, Marissa expected both side rooms opened onto the long porch that faced the water.

On closer inspection of the inviting porch, dark but for the light from the main room, she noted a couple of large covered bird cages just outside Riley's bedroom. The outside living space being comfortably furnished, she sat on one of two cushioned, rattan couches. A plush orange-and-white cat appeared from some hidey-hole and sprawled on the couch opposite. Birds and a cat. So dolphins weren't the only animals Riley cared for.

Marissa stared out to sea for several minutes, caught as always by the rhythms of the night. Wind whispering through the nearby palms. Waves lapping against the dock. Cat purring from where it sat staring at her, demanding attention.

"So who are you?" she asked.

"Spike."

Though she jumped at Riley's sudden reappearance, she chose not to comment on his stealth yet again. "Odd name for a cat," she said instead.

Dressed in cutoffs and a worn T-shirt, his feet bare, he set down a tray on a rattan chest that served as a coffee table. "You don't know this guy." He leaned over and ruffled the cat's fur. "Spike's a tough one."

"Like his master?"

"He could take lessons." Rather than joining the feline, he sat next to her, making the couch seem too small for comfort. "I hope you like ice tea and home-made apple pie."

A forbidden thrill shooting through her at the near contact, she protested, "You don't need to feed me."

"I don't do anything—"

"I know," she interrupted, finishing for him, "that you don't want to do."

"Now you're learning." He lit a couple of candles set in hurricane-lamp-style holders.

She had a long way to go to learn enough about Riley O'Hare to feel as if she knew him. If she wanted to know him. Marissa reminded herself that she wouldn't be around long enough to accomplish such a feat. But as they shared the night and tea and pie, part of her couldn't help but wish she had the time.

Against all reason—not to mention common sense—she seemed to be developing a taste for dangerous men.

MARISSA HAD NO IDEA she was playing a dangerous game merely by being here. She really thought the deadly snake turning up in her shower and her getting locked in the freezer had been unconnected. Weird accidents. He didn't think she was stupid, merely too trusting. Naive.

That made her all the more attractive, Riley admitted. And definitely dangerous to him.

He knew he had no business inviting her into his home. He should have seen her to the door of her cabin and sent her packing in the morning as he had planned.

If she would go...

Somehow he doubted it. She might have a soft quality that appealed to him, but she was tough, possibly as tough as old Spike. When it came to what she considered her responsibility, she definitely had a one-track mind. He doubted she would leave until she was certain Kamiko was okay.

"So what drew you to dolphins?" he asked after swallowing his last bite of pie.

"Swimming with them. My dad ran a dive shop and took tourists out on excursions."

"And you went along."

"From the time I was a kid," she affirmed. "I loved the reef with all its beautiful creatures. But dolphins...they were magic for me. Dad seemed to know exactly where to find them. On my thirteenth birthday, he took me out, just the two of us. And the dolphins. An unbelievable experience. I was hooked."

"Don't you think that experience was unbelievable because the dolphins were free?"

"I know we don't agree on marine mammal ethics—"

He was quick to interrupt. "Look, I'm not trying to start an argument. I'm just asking for your real, heartfelt, gut-level opinion."

She was silent for a moment as if gathering her thoughts. Finally she said, "If all things were equal, then maybe all dolphins should be free. But man has always been a predator, has always been responsible for their deaths, whether by accident using purse seines or drift nets in his search for tuna...or purposely as in Japan where dolphin meat is considered some kind of delicacy."

Wishing he could ignore the first reference—dolphins caught in the tuna nets literally drown because they can't surface to get the air that every marine mammal needs—Riley considered the second. For years, the waters of Futo Harbor ran red with the blood of Dall's porpoises driven to shore and beaten to death with clubs by so-called fishermen. Forty thousand were killed in 1988, and the catch was curtailed by the Japanese government only because their numbers had dwindled so severely that they were approaching extinction.

"If we can't make the world care," Marissa was saying, "things will never change."

"And you think change is possible?"

"If I didn't, life would be pretty bleak. I can always hope for the best. I always try to."

Candlelight softened the angles of Marissa's face, making her almost as beautiful on the outside as she obviously was on the inside. Riley tried to steel himself against her. Against the feelings she roused in him against his will. If he was crazy for letting her into his house, what did that make him for thinking about letting her into his life?

He'd let Dori in, and she had betrayed him....

But Dori would never betray a man again.

"So you see," Marissa was adding, "we actually don't think all that differently."

"Not about the basics, no. Just in what we choose to do about our beliefs."

"I'm not opposed to the refuge," Marissa insisted. "This place serves a real need . . . though it could use a lot of sprucing up."

Riley tamped down his instant irritation at the criticism. "We do what we can with the money we have." And, unfortunately, Dori had seen to it that things were desperate, when before they'd merely been tight.

"But you could raise the money if you weren't so averse to publicity. If more people knew about Dolphin Haven, you could get more donations and make the needed repairs, maybe even expand your operation."

"I don't like publicity," Riley said stiffly. In fact, he avoided it like the plague, fearing nosy reporters would sniff out a story he didn't want to see in print—one that could destroy everything he'd worked so hard to build. "That's not why I do what I do."

"You could use a little loosening up in your attitudes," Marissa told him.

Riley was seeing through a light haze of red when he said, "You have no idea why I feel like I do!"

"You could tell me."

"And you could mind your own business," he said through clenched teeth.

Marissa looked stunned, almost as if he'd hit her. "I don't get you. You invite me into your house, you start this conversation, and now you're acting like I'm sticking my nose where it doesn't belong."

"Exactly."

"Did anyone ever tell you that you're an arrogant fool?"

"I'm sure you'd be glad to do the honors."

"You're impossible."

"Pigheaded?" he suggested, illogically torn between anger and amusement.

"Illogical."

Color suffused her face, softening it, making him soften toward her. "That's the best you can do?"

"Try pompous."

"I kind of like pompous." And he liked her, even though she hit a few too many nerves for comfort.

"How about crude?"

"How about it?"

Appearing utterly frustrated, Marissa shook her head. "How any woman could put up with you... Dori must have been a saint."

"Believe me, Dori was no saint." His mood darkened once more. "And I don't want to talk about her."

"You really are a control freak."

"When it comes to my private life, I have a right to be."

"When it comes to anything involving you, you mean." Rising, Marissa smiled sweetly and said, "So I guess we have nothing more to talk about."

Before he thought about what he was doing, Riley grabbed her wrist and jerked it so that she fell toward him. "Then let's not talk."

MARISSA TRIED TO CATCH herself—her hand shot out toward the back of the couch to stop her momentum—but Riley was faster, dragging her down against him before she could regain her balance. And, before she could protest, his arms snaked tightly around her, pinning her against him. Her struggle was half-hearted, the attraction she'd been trying to ignore suddenly in full bloom. She felt alive. Physically alive. Every inch of flesh, every nerve ending, responded to being pressed up against the man for whom she had so many ambivalent feelings.

And when he wrapped a hand around her neck and dragged her head closer to his, she stopped fighting altogether. She stopped breathing, too, as if forgetting the need for air. His mouth took hers as if it had a right to. She couldn't still the excitement, couldn't help herself from returning the kiss, from gladly accepting the tongue that invaded her so boldly. She wanted more.

When his hand found her breast through the thin cloth of her sundress, the breath she'd been holding exploded into his mouth. He moaned, shifting so that she lay across his lap, her thigh pressing into his quickening flesh. Another moan, deeper. His fingers stroked her nipple, played it until the delicate flesh hardened with a desire that telegraphed through her, hot and urgent.

Marissa felt as if the room were shifting...moving in smooth, dizzying waves...as if she were being dragged to some inexorable fate that she could not change...as if she were drowning....

Drowning!

Suddenly Dori's water-bloated face came between them.

Panicked by the unwelcome vision, Marissa ended the kiss, flattened her hands against his chest and pushed, but Riley would not free her. She was breathing hard. And she was furious. With him. With herself. For even now, she couldn't stop her physical response to him. Even thinking about finding Dori—his ex-lover—couldn't extinguish the sexual charge she'd recognized from the first.

"Having second thoughts?" he asked gruffly.

"Second, third, fourth—"

"I get the picture." And even as Riley finally freed her, Marissa noticed a furtive movement in the doorway. "Luke?" she whispered, rising to her feet.

Riley turned, and rather than greeting his son with some semblance of affection, asked, "How long have you been standing there?"

"Long enough."

The boy's terse words were an accusation. Marissa had never been so uncomfortable—or embarrassed—in her life. She wished she could slide out of the place without either father or son noticing.

"What is it?" Riley asked coolly.

Luke aimed hostile glares at them both. "Forget it!" And he stomped away abruptly.

"Maybe you should go after him," Marissa suggested.

"He's acting like an infant. Again. I have nothing to explain or to apologize for."

"But he's obviously upset."

"He gets upset about everything I do." Riley sighed and shook his head. "He'll get over it."

And so would she. "I'll be leaving now."

His gaze pinned her. "Because of Luke?"

"Because of you."

He didn't try to stop her. Rather than backtracking through the living room and kitchen, Marissa used the screen door at the side of the porch to avoid running into the teenager. She couldn't believe how cold Riley had been to his son. How insensitive...just as her own father had been insensitive to his family's needs.

Riley O'Hare was the last man on earth she should be attracted to. So why was she? Hormones weren't reasonable, that's why. They didn't make sense.

Marissa passed the food-preparation building. That Riley's arrival had been awfully providential again occurred to her. Two days in a row they'd argued, and twice something odd and threatening—and potentially deadly—had happened to her. It had to be a coincidence, a weird twist of fate. Or stroke of luck for her. But what if it wasn't? And another, more dreadful thought occurred to her.

What if Riley and Dori had argued before she'd left for the oceanarium the night she'd died?

Chapter Six

The question wouldn't leave Marissa alone. It nagged at her all night. Plagued her in the morning. She dragged herself to breakfast late. The others had finished eating and were already heading out to work with the dolphins, Luke taking a fast lead, jogging toward the food-prep building, Riley at the tail.

"Morning." As if nothing had happened between them the night before, he nodded politely when he passed her.

Responding in kind—and ignoring the quickening inside her—Marissa wondered what the others would think when they saw the freezer door. Would Riley tell them what had happened? If so, they'd probably have a good laugh at her expense. She was certain none of them had any suspicions concerning their boss.

Once on the deck, Marissa checked the leftovers. The crew had pretty well depleted the morning spread. A mug of coffee, a few slices of mango and the last banana muffin would have to do. She grabbed the morning newspaper and sat down. A few minutes later, she was caught up in an article about a legal action Ocean Watch was bringing against Marathon Fisheries for killing more than the legal number of dolphins in their tuna nets. She'd just gotten to owner Ward Strong's side of the story when Billie started cleaning up.

If she wanted to learn more about the owner of Dolphin Haven, maybe the housekeeper could help her. Not that Billie would say anything against him intentionally, for she was obviously loyal. Riley had said that Billie treated him like a son. But if she could only hit the right buttons...

Marissa abandoned the newspaper and left the table. Wedging a hip against the counter, she asked, "Did Dori start many arguments with Riley?"

The startled housekeeper almost dropped the mug she'd been setting on a tray. "She wasn't the arguing type. She was very slick, that one."

"Slick?"

Billie's eyes narrowed in disgust. "Knew how to play a man, get him to do what she wanted." She thunked another mug down next to the first.

"Like letting her take days off." A fairly innocent feat—not exactly grist for a case against her.

"Hah," was all Billie muttered, concentrating on collecting the dirty dishes.

So there was more. How much more? Enough to make Dori's former lover hate her enough to... Marissa said, "So you didn't like her. I don't think Vida did, either. Did Dori have *any* friends?"

"What's all this interest in a woman you didn't even know?" Billie's expression changed from suspicious to hostile. "And what's this about arguments? You trying to do that Detective Lujan's job for him? You trying to prove my Riley is guilty of something?"

Realizing that the housekeeper had, indeed, jumped to Riley's defense and that she seemed overly anxious to protect him, Marissa figured she'd better smooth things over.

"Actually, I was just trying to figure Riley out. One minute he's impossible. The next . . . well, he can be very charming."

Let the woman make of that what she would. Marissa wasn't about to go into specifics or tell the housekeeper what had happened the night before—how an argument had turned into something far more intimate. Though for all she knew, Luke may already have spilled the beans.

"I was merely wondering if it was just me who aggravated him, or if Riley was so...ambivalent...with all women," Marissa added when the housekeeper wasn't forthcoming.

"He's got a problem with trust, and who can blame him?" Billie responded.

Nothing new there, Marissa thought, though knowing *why* might give her some insights.

Before she could ask, Billie added, "Best you leave him be," as if she did know about the night before . . . and disapproved.

So was that a warning?

"I'll be leaving soon . . . to go back to my job," Marissa stated carefully.

In the meantime, she would keep her nose out of Riley O'Hare's business and avoid him as much as possible. She'd do something to relieve the stress that was growing by leaps and bounds. Diving—that was it. She hadn't gone exploring in far too long.

"Good," Billie was saying. "The sooner you leave, the better."

"Why? Do you think I'm like Dori or something?" Marissa prompted in a last-ditch effort to get Billie to open up about this trust problem.

"Haven't decided yet. Dori was an opportunist." Billie stopped what she was doing to glare at Marissa. "That description fit you? Are you another woman who'd latch onto Riley for everything he's got?"

Not that everything he had was much, thought Marissa, though she kept the observation to herself. "I'm more interested in people than in their possessions," she said.

"Humph." Loading the last of the dirty dishes onto her tray, the housekeeper headed for the half-dozen stairs that led to the kitchen. On her way up, she turned and said, "You'd do well to leave now. Today. Before . . ."

Billie didn't finish. She left the statement dangling. Ominously. Marissa rubbed the goose bumps on her arms. *Had* the woman been threatening her or not? Was she so protective of Riley that she didn't want to see him with any woman?

More importantly—had Wilhemina Van Zandt disliked Doris Lynch enough to want her dead?

MARISSA FELT RILEY'S GAZE on her most of the morning as he and Ken worked with the four adult dolphins on some experiments combining echolocation skills with reasoning. He would show them a small sheet of metal, then show them first two, then three sheets of different metals at the same time, hoping to get them to identify the original.

They all did so without fail.

Even being familiar with the incredible intelligence of marine mammals, Marissa was impressed.

Then a little before noon, the experiments finished for the morning, Ken left with Vida to do some chores around the grounds. Luke had disappeared to who knew where an hour before. So she was alone with Riley, technically speaking, except for the dolphins, of course. She was sitting on the boardwalk of Kamiko's pen, scratching the dolphin's stomach, when Riley refused to let her ignore him any longer.

"I could use your help."

"*Mine?*" Remembering Vida telling her that Riley held the fact she'd worked as an assistant trainer in a zoo against her in her quest for Dori's job, she asked, "Are you sure?"

"Positive. I need to take some blood from Anook, but she gets flustered if the other dolphins bug her in the process. Maybe you could distract them for me."

Keeping herself distracted from him was another problem.

Marissa kept Brutus, Lolly and Pegeen busy playing keep the plastic baseball bat away from the trainer while he tended to Anook. One of the first things marine mammals in captivity were taught was to cooperate during veterinary tasks. On his signal, Anook presented her tail fluke to Riley, who sat cross-legged on a float attached to the boardwalk. The dolphin patiently waited while Riley took the blood sample. It might take as long as a year of patient work before a dolphin or whale would allow blood to be drawn. He was incredibly gentle with Anook, and the mellifluous tone he used as he coaxed her to cooperate was sultry enough to get a human female to do anything he wanted.

Practically anything, Marissa amended.

Finally Riley signaled Anook that he was done. "Good girl."

The dolphin somersaulted and came up close to the floating jetty in the large pen, mouth open. Riley promptly rewarded her by scratching her tongue, then giving her the last few fish in her bucket.

"That's it, then," Riley told Marissa. "You can go back to Kamiko or whatever until lunch."

"I thought I'd skip lunch." That way she could spend less time around him, while taking part in her favorite activity. "Any decent diving around here?"

"The reef."

"Too far. I don't want to be gone all afternoon. I just need a short break."

"Try the bridges connecting the keys."

"How about Florida Bay?"

He shrugged. "Several years ago, an old fishing boat sank about two and a half miles straight west during a tropical storm. The wreck's only sitting in about thirty feet of water. *The Hardship*'s not teeming like the reef, but there's some coral growth and sponges, and a large enough variety of fish hangs around to make it interesting."

"Great. Can I borrow a skiff? And a tank?"

He seemed reluctant but finally said, "Sure. Who's diving with you?"

Vida and Ken and Luke all had to work. Hoping he wasn't going to insist on volunteering—the idea was to get away from him so she could unwind—she said, "No one."

"You think that's a smart idea?"

"It won't be the first time I've dived alone." Marissa said this knowing she was tempting fate. She had done it before, but always in familiar waters. "And this doesn't sound too dangerous."

"Diving is always dangerous."

She was well aware of that fact—her father had died on a dive.

But she was megacareful. And the way Riley said it made it sound like a threat. Another one. Her imagination was going full blast, had been for the past couple of days. Now she was even wondering if Riley's fifty-something housekeeper could have murdered a young, fit woman. She had to stop seeing boogeymen where there were none.

"Are you going to take back the offer of the skiff and tank?" she demanded to know.

He stared at her as if he was considering it, but in the end he shook his head. "Your life is your own."

"Good. We're agreed on something."

"See Vida when you're ready to leave. She'll get you what you need."

Knowing she couldn't wait until dinner to eat, Marissa made a detour on the way to her quarters, stopping at the restaurant to order a sandwich and soda to go. She could eat after the dive, on her way back in.

"I'll be back as soon as I change," she told Ansel after placing her order. "The fishing boat that went down in the storm—how exactly do I find it?"

"There's a buoy marking the spot. Can't miss it. Everyone around here knows it." He gave her an intense look. "You're not going alone?"

"Would I do something so foolish?" she hedged.

His eyebrows shot up, and she guessed he figured she would.

She turned to go, practically running into Cole Glaser, who must have heard every word of the exchange. He always seemed to be hanging around, watching, listening. Irritating her.

"Excuse me." When he didn't move, she went around him.

For some reason, she wasn't surprised when he followed her out the door and onto the path to the cabins. "We seem to be going in the same direction," he said, moving up alongside her. "So when are we going to share a dinner?"

"I never said I would."

"You never said you wouldn't. I thought you gave me a rain check the other night."

Wondering why he was so persistent, she hedged yet again. "I'll think about it. In the meantime, maybe you can tell me something." If he could be nosy, so could she.

"What's that?"

"What were you and Riley arguing about?"

"A personal matter."

Somehow Marissa doubted the two men were friendly enough to get personal, but she figured he wasn't about to be more specific.

"I thought Riley was going to do you bodily harm," she said.

"He wouldn't dare."

"How can you be so sure?"

"It wouldn't be in his best interests."

What kind of best interests?

Did anyone ever give a straight answer around here? Marissa was beginning to doubt it.

Relieved when Glaser turned off to a cabin a hundred feet from her own, she focused on her upcoming excursion. Thirty feet of water didn't necessitate a wet suit, but she'd rather be safe than sorry. Nothing like getting cold to ruin a dive. Besides, it would afford her protection in case she scraped against anything sharp.

Inside her quarters, she went straight to the closet where she'd hung up her diving gear. She took down her favorite warm-water wet suit—thin, legless and a brilliant blue mixed with a black design—and started to slip it on over her bathing suit. As she did so, something scratched her thigh. Glancing down while pulling the suit in place, she noticed a bit of dark metal imbedded in the black neoprene at her hip. Carefully she worked it out of the rubber-like material so as not to rip the garment, and came away with a tiny shark.

She recognized the artifact as being the logo of Predator, a manufacturer of diving equipment. But she didn't own any Predator equipment. No doubt the shark had come off another trainer's equipment at the oceanarium and had somehow made its way into her things. She'd find out who when she returned to work shortly.

Not that it was important.

Opening the top dresser drawer where she'd thrown the few accessories she'd brought, she slipped the tiny metal shark into the small zippered case containing a jumble of earrings she hadn't even worn yet. She took out her dive watch and fastened it on her wrist.

Grabbing her mask, regulator, buoyancy compensator vest, weight belt and flippers, she left the room, picking up the lunch she'd ordered on her way to the refuge.

Vida was waiting for her at the dock, where she was filling a tank. She looked up from her task. "That's yours for the afternoon," she said, pointing to the nearby skiff. "So you're going out to *The Hard-ship?*"

"Have you been there?"

"A couple of times." The blonde stood and easily shifted the tank into the boat. "It's pretty nice, though visibility would be better at the reef."

"I just need a little break." Marissa dumped her equipment next to the tank, checking for the Diver Down flag. "Working with a stressed-out dolphin all day is starting to stress *me* out." Not to mention the couple of good scares she'd had. "Maybe I'll do one of the reefs another day."

"Maybe I'll come with you. Ken's a terrible diving partner—doesn't even realize when he leaves you behind. And Billie's not exactly a fun person to dive with."

Uncertain that she wanted to spend time with the blonde, Marissa said, "Maybe, if our schedules click," not wanting to sound ungracious.

Vida gave her more explicit directions on how to get out to the wreck. And all the while, Marissa felt as if the eyes of the house were on her. Rather, someone inside, watching her from the second story. Billie? She saw movement, but couldn't make a positive identification through the dark screened porch. Self-consciously, she zipped up her wet suit and slipped into her buoyancy compensator. Properly inflated, the vest would keep her neutrally buoyant underwater and help regulate her ascent back to the surface.

Vida untied the boat from the dock and threw the line in to Marissa. "Well, I've got to get back before the guys polish off all the food."

"Have a good lunch."

With that, Marissa took off, aware that she was still under close scrutiny. And until she reached open water, she couldn't even begin to relax.

Boats of all types plied the waters of the bay, including Toby Hanson's craft. A couple of teenage boys honked the horn of the yacht that most likely belonged to one of their parents. All the while, she kept an eye on the compass and watched for several distant landmarks Vida had indicated. The buoy marking the wreck's location made it a snap to find.

After anchoring nearby, Marissa donned the rest of her gear and wasted no time in setting out her Diver Down flag before entering the water. As usual, the sea soothed her. It was a totally different, magical world underwater. The sun was bright, the bay calm. Visibility was forty, maybe fifty feet. The wreck sat directly below.

Adjusting her buoyancy compensator, breathing through her regulator, she slowly sank, her avid gaze taking in every nuance of the old boat lying derelict on the ocean's floor. Encrusting sponges, hydroids and the beginnings of coral growth already decorated the steel hull. And fish swam around and through door and window openings.

Moving closer, she passed parrot fish and grouper, snapper and jacks. Nearby, a six-foot ray silently glided inches above the sandy bottom. Distracted, she followed it awhile, eventually turning back to *The Hardship*.

Schools of fish suddenly scattered, and a shadow at the surface indicated the arrival of another boat near hers. It slowed but didn't stop for more than a few seconds, quickly picking up speed as it propelled away. The fish settled back down to their routine activities, and Marissa joined them, barely moving, allowing her body to drift between them, her eyes to absorb the brilliant colors. She was startled once when a barracuda shot out of an opening directly in front of her.

Time passed all too quickly. Her hour was up, and her pressure gauge indicated she was nearly running on empty. It was just as well. Exhaustion from a combination of exercise and too little sleep was setting in. She began her ascent.

But as she slowly rose, Marissa felt a growing sense of confusion. The sun was spotty but still lighting the surface, yet she could not identify the smudge that was her skiff's shadow. Maybe she was turned around. She stopped for a moment and circled in place, her gaze darting to every inch of water within her view. No dark spot.

She tried not to panic. She took her time and kept breathing so she wouldn't chance injury to her lungs. But her pulse went out of kilter. Blood pumped through her limbs as she rose to the surface.

"Oh, Lord, no!"

No skiff. Not anywhere in sight. No other boats close enough to hail, either. She was alone. Above her, dark clouds were rolling in. The water was getting choppy. A storm was brewing hours earlier than predicted. She'd been warned about diving alone, and she'd tempted fate, anyhow, maybe for the last time.

What the hell was she going to do now?

"Don't panic!" Should she lose control, she would certainly drown.

Marissa inflated her buoyancy compensator slightly to keep herself afloat without having to work at it. If the weather hadn't shifted, another boat would probably come by and rescue her, but as it was, she couldn't count on anything but herself and her own ability to swim nearly two and a half miles when she was already exhausted. What could have happened to the skiff? She'd anchored it securely, so how could it have worked itself free?

Unless it hadn't . . .

Heart in her mouth at what that thought conjured up, she used her watch's compass to set the proper course back toward Lime Key. Then she began swimming. Slow, easy strokes. Long kicks of her flippers propelled her through the water. If only she'd had a proper night's sleep. If only those storm clouds hadn't shown up hours earlier than predicted—they were practically overhead now, and it wasn't supposed to rain until sometime that evening.

Had whoever cut her anchor line known the storm was ahead of time? For she was certain the skiff's disappearance was no accident. Someone had deliberately sabotaged her. She remembered seeing the shadow of another boat stopping near her skiff. That must have been when it had happened.

That meant someone wanted her dead. But who?

The killer was the only answer that made sense. But why?

She hadn't seen anything. She was no threat to the guilty one. Or was she?

A wave hit her hard and she swallowed water, nearly gagging at the salty liquid forced down her throat. She adjusted the compensator once more to give her extra buoyancy. All that lay before her was more water. How much farther before she reached Lime Key, she wasn't certain, but she didn't think she'd swum over a half mile. How would she ever make two more? In the distance, she could see a boat, but there was no way she could signal it. She kept going. Thinking about why she was in this situation would have to wait until later.

She was concentrating on putting one arm in front of the other, on putting extra energy into each kick, when something bumped first one foot, then the other. Thrown off her rhythm, she wavered, then swallowed more water. She was coughing as she stopped swimming, and she hung suspended as she tried to catch her breath, hoping to God the thing assaulting her wasn't a shark.

A long body slid along hers. She wanted to scream until it came to the surface, seemingly grinning at her.

A dolphin!

"Where did you come from?" she gasped. Then she gave the animal a better look and recognized the rake marks on his side. "Brutus?"

In response, he made frantic clicking noises and, rising practically onto his tail fluke, backed away from her. When she didn't follow, he whistled, dived and circled her, coming so close he slid against her torso.

It finally dawned on her—he was offering help!

Marissa reached out and grabbed his dorsal fin. Brutus wasted no time in moving off. A moment later, they were cutting through the water at a speed far greater than any human could swim. And the sky above was opening. With a rumble, the rain began, soft splashes at first, but rapidly progressing to a downpour.

And Marissa could only thank God that the dolphin had found her. But how?

Squinting ahead, she spotted the boat again. Close this time. Brutus was heading straight for it—the boat from Dolphin Haven! Suddenly the engines cut, and the craft slid silently through the water, a figure in a black slicker bent over the bow.

Riley!

"Let him bring you around back to the dive platform!" he yelled against the thrust of the storm, giving the dolphin a hand signal even as he ran to the platform himself.

What was Riley doing out here, anyway?

The waves were heavier now, and getting up a ladder sunk in the water would be no piece of cake. Marissa wasn't certain she wanted to try—not only because she could get hurt in doing so, but because she could get killed if Riley was the murderer. But if he was the one who cut her anchor line, wouldn't he have left her to her fate while he rushed back to the refuge in order to have an alibi?

Riley quickly descended to the diving platform. Wanting to believe the best of the man, Marissa removed her tank and handed it up to him, then followed by doing the same with her flippers. Brutus stayed with her until she grabbed hold of the railing. Then, timing her lunge upward to correspond with a wave, she found a solid footing.

Riley's face was wreathed in a dark expression, one she could not read. His green gaze was equally dark and it burned into her, making her hesitate....

The next thing she knew, Riley had hold of her wrist and was pulling her up. She couldn't fight him even if she wanted to. And fight for what? To let the sea take her, perhaps forever? He kept her going up the ladder to the deck, handing her the tank and flippers, which she secured against the side of the boat. Finally he ascended, and once facing her, pulled her straight into his arms.

He held her tight against his chest for a moment, the rain beating down on them both. Heart pounding, she allowed it, though her feelings were still mixed. For a third time, he'd appeared exactly when she'd been in trouble.

Coincidence number three?

"You could have drowned out there," he murmured into her hair.

Exactly.

So why didn't she fight him when he bent his head to kiss her?

Marissa responded as if she trusted him completely. She couldn't help herself. Maybe it was an affirmation of being alive...maybe it was purely gratitude...maybe it was sheer lust...but she gave herself over to emotion and physical sensation. She wanted him, and at that precise moment, he could have taken her right on the deck—rolling sea, rain and all.

And so, seconds later, when he pushed her toward the cabin, saying, "Get inside," she was surprised. And disappointed.

Glancing over her shoulder, Marissa saw him signal Brutus to return home. Rather than be alone in the cabin below, she followed him under the open canopy sheltering the wheel.

"Why aren't you where you can get warm?"

She realized she was shaking, but it was more from the experience than from being cold. "Why are you—and Brutus—out here?"

"Looking for you." He gave her that burning look. "What the hell happened to the skiff?"

"Your guess is as good as mine." She figured he could take that any way he wanted.

He stared at her for a moment and then, cursing, started the engine. Obviously he had taken it in the very worst way. Once the boat was moving, he turned it in an arc back toward Lime Key. Marissa almost felt guilty. Almost.

She was in lust. That didn't mean she wasn't rational. She just didn't know what to think.

"I had the weather channel on and heard the storm was ahead of schedule," Riley finally said, his tone gruff. "I figured you could be in trouble, so I came out to warn you."

"With a dolphin?"

"Brutus was up to his old tricks. When he saw me take the boat out, he decided to come along for the exercise."

"You didn't try to take him back?"

"There wasn't time. And if he wanted to take off, I would wish him well. I've tried setting him free before, but he always comes back."

"Home," she said, seeing Lime Key through the rain. "How did he know to look for me?"

"Your flippers."

"What?"

"When I spotted you at a distance, I knew you were in trouble, and I figured he'd get to you faster than I would, so I showed him a flipper, set him in the right direction, and told him to fetch."

Nerves suddenly collapsing, Marissa laughed. Playing fetch with a dolphin, her being the catch. It was pretty funny. So funny, she was almost hysterical.

When she got herself back under control, he again asked, "So what happened to the skiff?"

And this time she answered straight. "I think someone cut the line."

"Someone?"

"Dori's murderer." He didn't seem surprised. That got to her. She didn't want to believe he'd had anything to do with it. She watched him closely when she added, "I think Dori's murderer tried to kill me."

But he didn't react; he merely said, "Again. The coral snake was a good touch. Believable even though I've never seen one on this particular island before. But your getting locked in the freezer the very next night..."

She'd come to the same conclusion. So why did her heart pound so hard hearing him say it? She guessed she wanted someone to tell her she was crazy—or at least that she was letting her imagination run wild.

Part of her was afraid. A bigger part was angry. How dare some creep think he could play around with her life, not once, but three times. No doubt he would try again. And no doubt he thought he wouldn't get caught. If it was the last thing she ever did—she cringed at her own phrasing—she would finger the guilty one and put him behind bars!

The rain had let up to a drizzle by the time they docked the boat. Brutus circled the water outside his pen, stopping every so often to complain loudly. Since the other staff members had disappeared—presumably they'd taken shelter against the weather—Marissa insisted on helping Riley with the dolphin. In the water to work with the fencing, she gave Brutus a big hug and kiss on the nose before letting him rejoin his harem in the pen.

Afterward, as they dripped along the soaking-wet boardwalk, Riley said, "Your place or mine?"

Not in the mood to socialize—her disposition matching the stormy gray skies—she said, "All I want to do is get cleaned up." She didn't trust herself to be alone with him, not after the events on the boat. Not now, when she was at her most vulnerable.

His piercing gaze cutting through her defenses, Riley insisted, "We have to talk. We have to decide what to do about this."

She knew he was right. She couldn't ignore the situation any longer. Someone was out to get her and wouldn't stop until he'd succeeded. "Give me half an hour."

Riley nodded. "I'll be at your place in exactly thirty minutes. Be careful."

"I'm sure whoever set the skiff free expects I'm floating around in the bay."

"The island has eyes," he said mysteriously, which spooked her so that she kept glancing over her shoulder all the way back to her quarters.

Her mind was equally busy. Why would the murderer want to kill her? Did he think she'd taken some kind of clue off Dori's body or something?

It wasn't until she was in her cabin, stripping off the wet suit, that she remembered the last time she'd worn it—the very night Dori had died!

Slowly she sank to the bed, gripping the wet suit in both hands, thinking. She was remembering how she'd been so intent on scanning the ocean for some sign of Kamiko that she hadn't realized a swimmer was riding in on the surf until they'd collided....

Stopped cold, Marissa gasped, "Sorry," as she flew off balance and fell to the pebbly wet sand, a heavy weight crashing down on her.

The swimmer was wearing scuba gear, and something sharp on the equipment had snagged her own wet suit, for the moment attaching them at the hip. Then rough hands shoved between their bodies, quickly freeing them. Without saying a word, the masked diver gathered the flippers on the sand and practically ran over her in an equal rush. Shaking her head at the rude behavior, Marissa stared for a second as the person removed the tank without slowing....

The murderer? Had she not only seen him but grappled with him, as well?

Without further analysis of the events, she went to the dresser and removed the zippered pouch holding her earrings. She dumped the contents onto the dresser top and found the shark. If she was correct, this could be a clue to the guilty party's identity!

She wanted to run out and show the tiny metal shark to everyone, but something held her back. Caution. Right now, the murderer was playing games with her. Deadly games, true. But he couldn't be certain she remembered anything, so he was being cautious, staging "accidents" that no one could trace to him. Or her, she added, thinking of how both Vida and Billie had disliked Dori.

If she went public with the information ...

Choosing to play for time, Marissa slipped the shark back into the pouch.

Chapter Seven

"Where did Dori live?" Marissa asked Riley shortly after he arrived on her doorstep.

"In one of the bungalows, south of the pens."

She'd seen the grouping of small buildings set back in the trees, but she'd never been in one. "Maybe we should check it out."

"Detective Lujan went through the place thoroughly."

"He could have missed something. Or not known what to look for."

"And you do?"

"No." She didn't have the faintest idea; she was merely grasping at straws. "But maybe we'll find something, anyway."

Though not enthusiastic, Riley didn't object. The two things they had agreed on in the few minutes he'd been there was that she had to take these "accidents" seriously, and that they couldn't just sit around waiting for the next mishap to try to catch the murderer.

On their way, they passed Vida and Ken, who were back working with the dolphins. Riley's employees waved and gave them curious looks, but didn't voice any questions about what was going on. The workers' bungalows appeared as drab as the rest of the refuge's buildings. But inside, what had been Dori's place wasn't very different from her own rented cabin—a big bedroom with a sitting area and kitchenette decorated with casual rattan furniture.

This bungalow, however, had an inside shower.

"I'll start in the bathroom," Riley said. "You go through the closet and drawers."

Once a control freak, always a control freak, Marissa groused to herself, though she didn't object aloud. Searching through Dori's things *had* been her idea, after all. But without Riley's cooperation, she would still be stewing over the notion.

She looked around carefully, trying to get a more intimate picture of Doris Lynch. Lots of personal touches revealed a romantic side of the dead woman that didn't go with the image of the grasping man-eater Billie had described. Gauzy curtains and spread draped over the bed. Ruffled pillows. Nicely framed photographs on the chest of drawers. There was one of Dori and Riley, their arms wrapped around each other's back.

Refocusing on the task at hand, Marissa went through each drawer carefully, but learned nothing more revealing than the dead woman's taste in underwear and accessories, bathing suits, shorts and T-shirts.

"Nothing in the bathroom," Riley said matter-of-factly as he reentered the main room. "I'll check the kitchen cabinets."

Marissa felt uncomfortable snooping into someone's private life and wondered how Riley could be so emotionless about going through his former lover's things.

Starting on the closet, she asked, "How long ago did you break up with her?" She waited for an answer while going through a few dresses and skirts, pants and fancy shirts.

"About three months ago."

"Were you in love with her?"

A moment's silence was followed by, "I was 'in like.' I cared about her."

Dori had stored her diving gear in the closet, too. "Then why the breakup?" Nothing with the Predator logo, Marissa noted. Not that it should matter—Dori hadn't killed herself.

"She couldn't be trusted."

There it was again—the reference to Dori's being something less than honorable.

Truth to tell, she didn't trust Riley, not completely. Not enough to let him know about the scuba diver and the metal shark she'd found in her wet suit. She felt a little like she was cheating, playing a game without letting him know all the rules. But what if all those little chills she'd felt when around the man—the ones *not* caused by her hormones—had been right on. Not that she really believed it.

But what if...

Wandering from the closet to the bed, she checked the nightstand, which had on top a box of tissues and a romance novel. *A romance novel.* Picking up the book, she sank to the mattress.

Would a calculating man-eater really read about some fictitious woman's romantic escapades? Wouldn't she be more likely to gobble up a nonfiction book called *How to Get Your Man?* Or maybe *Starting Your Own Financial Empire Using Some Poor Sucker's Money?*

Flipping through the thick novel, Marissa stopped at the spot marked with a piece of gray notepaper. She was reading a passage highlighting the emotional conflict of the lovers when she felt Riley's presence. He was standing over her, looking every inch the part of the brooding hero in the book. Her heart skipped a beat.

"What did you find there?"

"Dori's choice in popular fiction." His presence disturbingly potent, she glanced away from him to take a better look at the notepaper used as a bookmark. "Hmm. A missive from someone. 'Must see you,'" she read, pulling out the note and letting the book close. "'Meet me at the cabin at midnight. Don't tell anyone, please, not before we have a chance to talk.' No signature." She challenged Riley's unemotional green gaze. "Meet who? You?"

"I never wrote her any such note. Let me see."

Marissa handed him the small slip of paper and returned the book to the nightstand. "Do you recognize the handwriting?" It was distinctive. Very clear and open, the caps decorated with loops and flourishes.

He shook his head. "Not really. This looks like a woman's handwriting to me."

"You think she was having a tryst with another woman?"

"This doesn't say anything about a tryst. Just that someone had to talk to her."

Someone who wanted Dori dead? "This could be significant. A clandestine meeting. About some secret?" she asked, reiterating Mrs. Lynch's claim to the detective. "Some big secret having to do with the refuge?"

His expression darkening, Riley said, "I think it's time to head north to Miami."

Immediately put off—wondering what exactly he had to hide that he changed the subject so abruptly—Marissa insisted, "I'm not going anywhere until I'm certain Kamiko has settled in." She popped off the edge of the bed to face him, trying not to let herself be affected by his nearness. "I haven't even let her in with the other—"

"Not you, us," he interrupted, stopping her blathering cold. "To see Detective Lujan."

"Why?"

"Isn't the fact that someone's been trying to kill you reason enough?" he demanded, almost poking his face in hers. "Maybe Lujan can assign you a guard."

With the warmth of his breath feathering her face, she tried edging back but had nowhere to go—the mattress was pressing into her legs. "I don't want some bodyguard following me around, shadowing my every move."

"You'd rather take a chance with your life?"

Thinking of that afternoon's escapade, she said, "No, of course not. But now that I know someone is after me, I'm forewarned, right? I can be extra careful. Besides, if some bodyguard was tailing me around, the murderer would assume that I knew something for sure and then wouldn't be so cautious in trying to keep me quiet."

"That sounds like a credible motivation. So, *do* you know something?"

A poor liar, Marissa swallowed and hesitated a fraction too long before saying, "No, not a thing." The pulse in her throat beat furiously.

And she sensed Riley didn't believe her. She squirmed inside as he edged closer. Tempted to spill her speculations about the scuba diver who'd left behind what she figured was a pretty important clue, she nearly had to bite her tongue to keep her silence about the metal shark.

Had to remind herself that she didn't fully trust Riley O'Hare.

Had to remember that raging hormones didn't have any sense, and that's why she felt as if she were on fire though Riley wasn't even touching her. His closeness... that steamy look he was giving her... what if this was all just for effect? To make her putty in his hands?

One of those hands was reaching for her, sliding around her neck.

Feeling only too pliable, she mustered all her willpower to force herself around him and toward the door. Once there, she glanced back. "Well?" She hoped he wouldn't notice how breathless she was.

He swallowed what sounded like a growl and followed.

"SO WHY DO YOU THINK someone's trying to kill you?" Detective Nick Lujan growled as he twirled the glass of mineral water, a sign of his impatience.

Marissa could hardly blame him for being testy. He'd been called away from dinner, and from the slick way he was dressed, she suspected he'd been with a date. For some reason, Riley had insisted they meet on neutral ground rather than either the refuge or the police station. Lujan had suggested this hotel bar in the Art Deco District of South Miami Beach. The place was lovely, a study in gray and mauve with marble-topped tables.

Unfortunately, the atmosphere didn't make what she had to say any easier. The wine spritzer, however, did.

"On each of the last three days, I've had what would have been viewed as unfortunate accidents, if I'd died." Marissa's mouth went dry even as she thought about it. She took another sip of her drink. "First, a coral snake got into my outdoor shower."

"You find them around, especially in the Keys," Lujan said.

"Though I've never seen one on Lime Key before," Riley countered.

"The point is, I didn't suspect anything," Marissa went on. "The same with the freezer incident. I was getting fish for my dolphin from the walk-in freezer... when the door swung shut."

"But there's a safety handle on those things."

"Which broke off in my hand. If it hadn't been for Riley here coming to my rescue—"

"You woulda been a Popsicle," the detective finished, giving Riley a measuring look. "You said three days?"

Marissa nodded. "Earlier today, I was diving at a wreck site, and when I came to the surface, my skiff was gone."

"You were diving alone?"

Sick of being criticized about the issue, she snapped, "That's not the point!"

She immediately felt Riley's hand slide over her knee. She supposed he was trying to be comforting, but his effect on her was anything but. She shifted in her seat and gave him a penetrating look. The hand stayed put.

"Sure you anchored the boat properly?" Lujan was asking.

"Uh, positive." Having difficulty paying attention, she glared at Riley, who was pointedly ignoring her. She did her best to disregard him and concentrate on the detective. "And while I was underwater, I saw another boat draw close and stop just for a moment. I didn't think any more of it until mine came up missing."

"Who knew you were going out to the site?"

"I did," Riley volunteered, finally removing his hand and leaning forward, folding his arms on the tabletop. "I told her about it. And I had Vida Dalberg get the tank and the skiff ready, so she knew."

"As did Ansel Roche, owner of Lime Tree Resort," Marissa added. "And one of the other guests overheard me talking to Ansel. His name's Cole Glaser."

She was aware of Riley's reaction, though he tried to minimize it. He'd seemed startled. And worried.

"That's it?" Lujan asked.

"What about Billie?" She scrutinized Riley. "Someone was watching me from the house."

"How do you know it wasn't me?"

"Was it?" she challenged him, wondering why he would cover for the housekeeper.

Detective Lujan cut through the instantly charged atmosphere. "Anyone else?"

She tore her gaze away from Riley. "Toby Hanson. I passed his boat as I was heading out to the site."

"So pretty much everyone on Lime Key knew."

"Seems like it, doesn't it?"

"Any ideas of who the guilty party might be?"

It was then that she should have told him about the incident on the beach, about the Predator shark the scuba diver had left imbedded in her wet suit. She should suggest he get a warrant and search every building on Lime Key until he found the piece of diving equipment missing its trademark logo. Maybe if Riley hadn't been there, she would have.

But he was and she didn't.

"No idea whatsoever." At least that was the truth.

She only hoped she was wrong to distrust Riley. She only prayed her hormones weren't working under false assumptions—that they weren't so free-spirited that she would be attracted to a murderer.

"I'd like to offer you protection, but the way things stand, I can't," Lujan said. "But maybe removing yourself from the situation would be your best bet for now."

"Removing myself?"

"By going home. If you're afraid, you should."

"I'm not about to turn tail and run out on my responsibilities," she said. "I'll leave when my job on Lime Key is done."

Why did she get the feeling that everyone would be happier if she left the island and returned home?

"You know something," Lujan said definitively, making her start. "Even if you can't quite remember what."

Having feared he was going to demand she tell him whatever it was that she was hiding, Marissa hoped her relief wasn't too obvious. "I suppose the killer must think so, too."

"I'd say your being able to finger him is reason enough for him to want you dead."

Marissa was relieved when Detective Nick Lujan left the bar a few minutes later, his glass of expensive water untouched, his vow to contact her the next day sounding more like a threat than a promise.

It took her awhile longer to realize that she wasn't the only one holding something back. "You never gave him the note we found."

"I forgot."

She only hoped that that was the truth and that Riley wasn't trying to protect someone.

RILEY WONDERED how much longer he could protect the refuge. Every time he turned around, he seemed to be thwarted. The way things were going, the truth was bound to come out.

Marissa was definitely suspicious.

"Want another drink?"

"No, I'm already feeling this one."

"A wine spritzer?"

"Some people would call me an easy drunk."

He remembered Billie suggesting he should keep Marissa happy by schmoozing her. He wouldn't mind keeping her happy, and it wouldn't be by schmoozing her, either. In a matter of days, he'd gone from being mildly to wildly attracted to her. As far as he was concerned, she was a goner, too. She could hardly keep her eyes off him, and he easily read the hunger in those deep blue pools. Half the time, the only thing on his mind was when they were going to do something about it.

The other half, he was preoccupied with murder.

"Maybe we should get going, then," he suggested, thinking that if he hadn't completely assuaged Marissa's suspicions, he'd made a dent in them by insisting on the meeting with Detective Lujan.

"Sounds good."

But as she rose, she swayed a little and clutched the table for support. "Oh!"

"Hey, easy." He put a steadying arm around her.

"I shouldn't have had that drink on an empty stomach," she said, taking a big breath. "I haven't eaten since breakfast, and that was next to nothing." Of course she hadn't eaten. She'd left her lunch on the skiff. And then he'd dragged her off to the mainland without thinking about getting some food in her first. A situation easily corrected—and one that he might be able to use to his advantage.

"We're getting you something to eat, pronto," he insisted, nudging her toward the door.

"You won't get any argument from me."

He took her to SeaDelights, a nearby restaurant on a side street off Collins Avenue. In season, the small place, decorated like the inside of an Art Deco cruise ship, would be crowded, but tonight several tables were available. He ordered a sampler platter of shellfish for two and asked the waitress to bring the salads and bread immediately.

Marissa hardly waited until the basket of warm rolls was set on the table before snatching one and taking a bite. "Mmm, I feel like I haven't eaten in weeks."

"Exercise can do that to you. Not to mention a healthy dose of fear. Do you dive solo often?"

Her smile stiffened. "Hardly ever."

Though he sensed it was becoming a sore subject with her, he couldn't let it alone. "Care to tell me why?"

"A challenge, I guess."

"You want to see how many times you can dive solo without getting yourself killed?"

She winced and said, "My father wasn't diving alone, but he died, anyway."

"I'm sorry."

"Not as sorry as I am."

The conversation was put on hold for a moment when the waitress brought their salads. Riley waited until Marissa had taken the edge off her hunger before continuing.

"I'd think your father's death would make you a more careful diver."

"I am careful. But having another person along is no guarantee...."

Recognizing the raw emotion in her expression, he slipped a hand over hers. "How long ago did it happen?"

"Twelve years." She pulled her hand free as if she was afraid to let him touch her. "You'd think I'd be over it by now."

"We never forget the people we lose." Despite the rotten circumstances, he doubted he would ever forget Dori.

"I was eighteen," Marissa was saying. "The first season Dad was going to let me dive for treasure with him."

"He was a sunken-treasure hunter?"

"Whenever he had the backing. In between stakes from wealthy investors, he ran the dive shop."

A normal state of affairs for treasure seekers. It took big money to mount such expeditions, and rarely did the person doing the hunting have it himself.

"His preoccupation with finding treasure must have been hard on your family."

"Mom hated his fixation. He was like Dr. Jekyll and Mr. Hyde. At times, he could be the most loving father and husband, but when he was on a hunt, everything but the promised treasure ceased to exist for him. Including us. My younger sisters barely got to know him." She gave him an odd look and added, "It's terrible when a man can place more importance on an obsession than on his own flesh and blood."

Why did he get the feeling she was sending him a message? Because he and Luke weren't real tight? He'd been trying his damnedest....

"Luke still buys into his mother's view of me," he told her. "A relationship takes work, and over the years, Cathy kept us from being together more than a few days or weeks at a time. Until now. Not that it seems to make much of a difference to Luke. He uses every chance he gets to let me know how much he still resents me."

"Maybe you need to make more of an effort with him."

"Maybe I would if I thought my advances would be appreciated."

"Maybe you have to take some chances."

"Like you do diving?"

She thought about it for a moment. "Exactly. Though to tell the truth, my experience this afternoon was enough to cure me of taking that particular chance again. From now on, I'll stick to the buddy system."

Thinking about how Dori had fooled him, he said, "We could all use someone to watch our backs at times."

Marissa looked as if she was about to ask him to explain, but the arrival of their shellfish platter—

grilled lobster, deep-fried shrimp, broiled scallops and panfried oysters—stopped her. Conversation abated while they did some serious eating.

And Riley did some serious watching. He liked Marissa's black hair loose around her bared shoulders. She was wearing a halter top and clam diggers in a brilliant blue that intensified the color of her eyes. With the low, warm light of the restaurant softening her features, she looked not only sexy as hell, but also beautiful.

Putting her fork down only after the platter was clean, Marissa made a face and groaned. "I'm so full I'm going to burst."

"Not in my car," Riley said with a chuckle, suddenly obsessed with the thought of getting her someplace where they could be alone. "We'll just have to walk it off."

A balmy night, a full moon, a stroll along the boardwalk—what could be more romantic? Riley called himself a fool. The last thing he needed to do right now was to get involved with another woman.

A woman who obviously knew more than was healthy for her to know.

A woman ripe for death.

DEATH SEEMED A distant concept as they walked north along the boardwalk, apartments and hotels on one side of them, beach and ocean on the other. The boardwalk was fairly new, installed well after the beach had been restored by moving tons of sand from the ocean's floor to rebuild the shoreline. A multitude of sea grape trees along the way not only provided shade during the day, but helped keep the beach from seriously eroding as it had done a couple of decades before.

Marissa dodged a kid who ran from his mother, but avoided getting too close to Riley. She was afraid of what might happen if she allowed it. Other couples strolled hand in hand or with arms wrapped around each other, while elderly people on benches—retirees—watched in approval.

One woman reminded Marissa of her mother, who'd grown old before her time, and she couldn't help asking, "So what kind of a relationship did you have with your parents?"

"Mixed. Like you."

"You worked with your father, too?"

"Never!"

The protest was so vehement it startled her. "What does your father do?"

"Can we talk about something else?"

She figured he didn't just mean the job issue. He didn't want to talk about his father, and his tone left no room for compromise.

For some reason, she couldn't leave it be. "You know, the relationship you had with your own parents probably affects the relationship you have with Luke."

"You're right. My father and I weren't close. We didn't agree on things. I don't respect him."

Don't—present tense. Then he was still alive, she realized. "But you love him, anyway."

"I'm not sure how I would classify the emotions I have for the man."

"What about your mother?"

"She's everything he isn't. I don't know how she could have stayed with him all these years. A misguided sense of loyalty, I guess."

"He...abused her?"

"No, of course not—not physically. But he has to control everything around him. Never could admit he was wrong."

Marissa gave him a meaningful stare.

Riley scowled. "He makes me look like a marshmallow. I do know how to compromise."

Marissa knew when to let well enough alone. Besides, it was too nice a night to spoil with an argument. When Riley suggested they leave the boardwalk for the beach, she gladly agreed, slipping out of her sandals and carrying them. He did the same with his loafers, rolling up the cuffs of his trousers, as well.

The tide was coming in. They made their way down to the ocean's edge and let the foaming waves roll in over their bare feet. The water was cold and invigorating. She squealed a little, but she didn't jump out of the surf.

She tried not to think of the last time she'd walked along this coast only a few miles north of here—of the night that Dori had died.

Gradually realizing Riley was holding her hand, Marissa thought she ought to do something about it— like free herself or, at the very least, discourage him from going any further. But something ignited between them on that quiet walk. Something she didn't want to ruin. Other than that first night, when she'd watched Riley swim with the dolphins in the moonlight, she hadn't seen him so relaxed. She liked this side of him. Easy. Comfortable. From what she could tell, unlike his father.

What had happened between father and son to put such a rift between them?

When Riley pulled her down to the sand just out of the water's reach, she was tempted to reintroduce the subject. Instinct stopped her. Instead, she asked how he'd started the refuge. A smart move. Riley was more than willing to talk about Dolphin Haven.

"It seemed the natural course when I left the navy," he told her, leaning back on an elbow. "With my experience, I couldn't think of doing anything but working with marine mammals."

Marissa leaned on her opposite elbow so they were both stretched out on the sand facing each other. "And you never considered working in a marine park or aquarium?" she asked, wondering if he'd always held them in contempt.

"I never finished the formal education most of those places required. Besides, I wasn't exactly the follower type. I learned that about myself in the military. That's why I didn't become a career man."

"So you wanted to be your own boss."

"Afraid so."

Obviously he'd always been a control freak of sorts. "And you were how old?"

"Twenty-six."

She did some quick calculations. "Then you were already a father."

"Luke was four or five when I started Dolphin Haven. Cathy hated it even more than she hated my being in the navy. She wanted me to go into business with—"

He stopped himself and Marissa guessed he'd been about to say she wanted him to go into business with his father.

"Cathy wanted me to have a real job," he went on. "One that paid real bucks."

While running an animal refuge was altruistic, it certainly wouldn't be profitable. "So she left you because of Dolphin Haven?"

"She only stayed long enough to convince herself that I wasn't going to change my mind. Too much work for too little money, she said."

Having lost a fiancé because of her dedication to her job, she said, "It would be a tough life for someone who doesn't love dolphins the way we do."

"Or for someone who loves money the way Cathy does. That was the real problem. When she hooked up with me, she figured she had it made."

Marissa supposed that that meant Riley's parents had money. Whatever business his father was in was obviously lucrative.

"Cathy found herself a more ambitious husband within months of leaving me," Riley went on. "Not that she was satisfied. That marriage didn't last more than a few years, either."

Either. Then he had definitely been married to Luke's mother. Odd that he and Luke had different last names. She couldn't see Riley letting his son be officially adopted by another man, but maybe Luke had taken his stepfather's name, anyway.

"So Luke's mother is single now."

"She's between husbands. She married and divorced a third time. Now she's hunting for number four, but it's hard work when each husband has to be wealthier than the last. And having a teenager around was becoming an inconvenience to her, so she finally let me have Luke for as long as I wanted. If I had my way, he'd never go back to her. But she is his mother and if he sees her faults, he ignores them."

"Maybe that's what he's had to do to be happy."

"That kid's never known real happiness. And I'm afraid there's nothing I can do to change that for him."

The catch in his voice got to her. Riley had real feelings for his son even if the two didn't always get along. Maybe he just didn't know how to deal with Luke because he hadn't had a good role model in his own father.

"At least you want to do something. That's the first, most important step," she insisted, reaching out to touch his hand. "Luke loves the refuge, and I'm sure he loves you, too. Make time for him. Make him believe he's the most important thing in your life, that you want to share your dream with him. Don't exclude him. I know what that's like. It was tough competing with some elusive sunken treasure, to see my dad so focused on some dream that he sometimes forgot I even existed for months at a time."

"I've never forgotten about Luke. I wanted custody, but back then I thought his being with his mother was the best thing for him. By the time I realized I was wrong, it was too late."

"It's never too late to convince someone you love them."

"I hope you're right."

Moonlight silvered Riley, casting a magical glow over the face that could seem so harsh at times. At the moment, his expression was sober...but hopeful. Heart beating a little faster, Marissa knew she was in trouble. Hormones were one thing; emotions another. His opening up like this about Luke hit her where she lived, big time.

So when he murmured, "I've never known anyone like you," and wrapped a hand around the back of her head, she didn't resist him.

Thrilled at his touch, she let him pull her closer. She let his lips touch hers in an exploration very different from the first time. This kiss was tentative and so all the more exciting, because he was taking nothing for granted. If she pulled away, she was certain he wouldn't try to stop her. Only she didn't want to pull away.

Riley rolled toward her, pressing her back into the sand. His body snuggled against hers and he deepened the kiss.

Marissa wrapped her arms around his neck and moved even closer into his heat. When he found her breast, she arched, pushing the sensitive flesh into the palm of his hand, pressing harder against the thigh wedged between hers. She hadn't felt so wild and uninhibited since...maybe never. After all, she hadn't known Riley O'Hare before.

He was loosening the buttons on her blouse, and she was helping him, when a wave rolled in over their feet, the cold water making her squeal. Pushing at his chest, she held him at bay for the moment. Her body still pulsed with desire and she was breathing hard. She wondered exactly how far she was willing to go with Riley O'Hare, a man she hardly knew. A man she wasn't sure she liked.

The hunger in his expression told her exactly what *he* wanted.

Flustered, she glanced away and watched another wave crash into the shore, implacably reminding her of Dori. Water-bloated face. Eyes staring blankly.

And the spell was broken.

Her mind cleared.

They were connected at the hip, Riley's weight pinning her to the sand...reminding her of the scuba diver who'd appeared out of the surf only to flatten her. A chill shot through her, and in her mind she relived the incident.

Determinedly freeing herself, Marissa scooted away from Riley. "We should be getting back." She straightened her clothes even as she got to her feet. What had she been thinking? Going further would have been madness.

"Right."

Riley stood, gathered up his loafers and started off toward the boardwalk, leaving her to play catch-up. His mood could turn so quickly....

Marissa stared at the straight back and the rigid set of his shoulders and visualized the scuba diver walking away from her. She raced after Riley, frantically trying to judge if he was the same size as the mystery man on the beach that night...and wondering if he owned any Predator equipment.

He was capable of great anger and even violence—his tussle with Cole Glaser was still clear in her mind. If only she knew what that had been about. He also seemed straightforward, not the kind of man to play games as someone had been doing with her.

Still, no matter how much she rationalized, the same question plagued her: was he capable of murder?

MURDER SHOULD BE EASIER.

Dori had gone down without much of a fight, but the Gilmore woman was another story. She seemed invincible.

Marissa Gilmore wasn't worthy of being the center of anyone's existence, but that's exactly what was happening. It was hard to think about anything else with her still around. A lesser soul would have given up—three strikes and you're out—but that wasn't possible here, because she was asking too many questions.

It was only a matter of time before she put things together and pointed an accusing finger.

Frustrated or not, the game had to continue.

And in the end, Marissa Gilmore would come up dead.

Chapter Eight

"Heard you had some trouble yesterday."

Startled by the unexpected intrusion into her session with Kamiko—she'd just allowed the dolphin to join the two females and the calf—Marissa nearly swallowed a mouthful of salt water. She treaded water and gaped up at Erasmus North, who squatted on the boardwalk looking as grizzled as ever.

"I lost a skiff out near *The Hardship,*" she conceded.

"Heard it was more like someone set it adrift and left you to drown."

Odd that he had sought her out to discuss the situation. She tried to read his expression beneath his billed cap, but Erasmus kept a poker face.

"Heard from who?" she asked. Had Riley been discussing her near miss with this man?

"Everyone knows about it."

No one had said a thing to her over breakfast, though. "It wasn't exactly an experience I'd want to relive."

"Don't have to." Erasmus ran a hand over his beard-stubbled chin. "You got another life away from here. You can go back to it and forget about this place before it's too late.''

Marissa was stunned. She'd barely spoken to the fisherman before, yet he seemed inclined to give her advice. A warning, really. Yet another person telling her to go home. Why? Had Riley put him up to it?

"I'll be leaving soon."

"Sooner the better. You don't want to end up like Dori.''

Dead? Her pulse suddenly thundered through her. "Do you know something I don't?''

Rising from his crouching position, he laughed. ''I imagine I do, considering the years I got on you.''

He was playing it light, but Marissa wasn't about to let him get off so easily. She quickly hiked herself out of the water and onto the boardwalk. Someone was trying to kill her and that made her bold. "You seem to know a lot about what's going on here. Maybe you know what happened the day before yesterday.''

She couldn't tell if his puzzled expression was genuine when he said, "Nothing comes to mind.''

"Funny, but I'm sure I saw you sneaking around the house in the dark…just before someone locked me in the dolphin chow freezer.''

''I wouldn't know about any of that," he said, a little too quickly for her taste.

And the poker face slipped a bit. Showing what? Surprise? Or guilt? Just as she was about to press him regarding the coral snake, she spotted Riley on his way to join them. Something made her clam up—maybe the same misgivings she'd had the night before.

Daylight did nothing to help shake her attraction to the man. Wearing dark glasses, a dive watch and a brief black swimsuit, he was definitely hot enough to make any healthy woman's libido sit up and take notice.

"Erasmus," Riley said, not bothering to hide his surprise, "thought you would have been long gone."

"Uh, routines get boring. You don't mind if I watch for a time, do you?" he asked, indicating Luke, who was working with the juveniles in the next pen.

"Go ahead. Luke likes showing off."

Erasmus moved away. Marissa was eyeing the gray-haired man when Riley said, "I'm taking the boat over to Key West in a little while. I thought you might want to come."

A bit daunted at the prospect of being alone with him again, she demurred. "I shouldn't leave Kamiko on her own."

He glanced down at the dolphin, who was quite happily interacting with the other two females. "She's not on her own. And she's doing fine."

"For now—"

"I'll tell Vida to come out of the office and keep an eye on her." She was trying to think of another excuse when he added, "I'm planning on paying Dori's mother a visit."

An excursion he knew she wouldn't be able to resist.

Marissa couldn't help noticing that while Erasmus North pretended interest in Luke and the juveniles, he had his head cocked in their direction and seemed to be listening to their every word. Instinctively she grabbed Riley's arm, and giving him a meaningful look to cease the conversation, she pulled him in the other direction.

Waiting until they'd gotten far enough away to satisfy her, Riley asked, "So what was that all about?"

She glanced back. "I don't trust him."

"Erasmus? What's not to trust?" Riley turned his gaze on the fisherman, who was now on his haunches talking to Luke. "He's been supplying the refuge with fish for years."

"*Someone* killed Dori," she reminded him, and before he could object to her implication, she asked, "Did you tell him about yesterday?"

"You mean your getting left out in the bay? The only person I discussed it with was Billie, and only because she had to make a claim with the insurance company."

"Erasmus knew."

Riley frowned. "Undoubtedly word got around. After all, you came back, but the skiff didn't."

"Let's talk about this later," Marissa suggested. "On the way to Key West."

They cast off within the half hour, having had barely enough time to change. Marissa wore a sleeveless purple crinkled cotton jumpsuit, and had gathered her hair into a ponytail. She'd also slipped on a pair of dangling seashell earrings taken from the zippered pouch. She'd held the metal shark in her hand for a moment and wondered what she was doing.

Not telling Detective Lujan everything. Playing Nancy Drew. She prayed that Riley would prove to be one of the Hardy Boys rather than the villain.

As the boat moved away from the dock, she scanned the island. Cole Glaser was standing in the shade of a palm tree near the restaurant, beer in hand, his attention focused on them until he was interrupted by Ansel Roche. The two men exchanged what seemed to be heated words. Then, abruptly, they retreated into the restaurant.

Was Cole running up a big tab or something?

Shaking off the speculation, Marissa decided to do a little probing as they headed into Florida Bay. "So, are you a fisherman?"

Riley gave her a surprised look. "Killing anything for sport never appealed to me. Why?"

"This is a pretty fancy boat. I just wondered if you used it for anything besides getting around the islands... or transporting dolphins."

"I do some scuba diving. Everyone at the refuge does. I never much liked diving off a small craft."

Knowing he was referring to the lost skiff, she said with sincerity, "I never will again."

They were silent for a minute, and Marissa's mind began working, trying to figure out an excuse to go exploring... to see what brands of diving equipment he carried on board.

When he asked, "Hungry?" a few minutes later, Marissa realized this was her chance. Billie had packed them sandwiches and cans of soda.

"I could use some food," she said, keeping her tone casual. "I'll get the stuff from the fridge after I, uh, visit the head." On the way there, she planned on finding the equipment storage area.

"No big rush."

Afraid of getting caught, she hurried through the cabin anyway, checking a couple of bench seats with storage underneath. One was filled with canned goods, the other with emergency medical supplies. A closet in the kitchen area yielded nothing but shelves of dishes and cleaning products.

Finally, opening a door next to the head, she was elated—success!

As she inspected the equipment, she kept looking over her shoulder, half-expecting Riley to check on her. She was relieved when he stayed out of sight.

The closet was jammed with wet suits of various sizes along with the accompanying gear. She sought out brand names. Techna. Dacor. Oceanic. Tabata. No preference for one brand of equipment. About to breathe a sigh of relief, she spotted it—a black buoyancy compensator jacket stuffed in the back. Fearful of what she would find, she held her breath as she pulled it away from the rack. The jacket was, indeed, a Predator...but its metal shark was still attached to the light pocket flap where it belonged. She let out her breath. And the jacket was only a medium, definitely too small for Riley.

She was relieved...and yet uneasy.

Someone at the refuge used Predator equipment. But who?

Thinking she might have overlooked something, her eyes swept the closet once more, but no other item sported the metal shark.

Still in deep thought, she closed the closet door—

And jumped when Riley yelled, "Hey, what's a starving man got to do to get lunch?"

"I'm coming!" She moved fast, quickly removing the sandwiches and cans of soda from the small refrigerator. Ascending to the deck, she said, "Sorry. I didn't mean to take so long."

Her nerves jittery at having searched through his things—at not having believed in him—she calmed down some when Riley turned a half-cocked smile at her and joked, "Thought you might have gotten yourself flushed down the head."

He checked his course, locked down the wheel, and spun toward her without leaving his seat. Marissa forced a smile to her lips, handed him his lunch, and sat on a bench close to him. She hoped he couldn't detect the guilt that was growing inside her. He'd saved her life. He'd insisted on her telling Detective Lujan everything. Though she hadn't. He was involving himself because of her.

So why did she hesitate telling him about the scuba diver? About the clue she'd found? Because she felt foolish now. Because she didn't want him to know how little faith she'd had in him when he'd gone all out for her.

It wasn't until they'd finished eating and Riley had his hands back on the wheel that he asked, "So what about Erasmus?"

She'd almost forgotten about the fisherman. "Supplying your dolphin chow all these years, he must feel like he has an investment in Dolphin Haven," she said, wondering if Erasmus was a diver, too. "Enough to deliver a warning."

"What?"

"He told me to go back to my own life before it was too late—before I ended up like Dori."

"Who the hell does he think he is?" Riley muttered more to himself than to her.

"I wouldn't have any idea. If you decide to find out, you can also ask why he was sneaking around your house the night I got locked in the freezer."

Riley's gaze suddenly bored through her. "Why didn't you tell me this before?"

"Before, I thought it was an accident."

"You knew better yesterday."

"I had a lot on my mind yesterday."

And not just the attempts on her life—Riley himself had been a great distraction. Dressed in jeans that fitted like a glove, he was distracting her now. No matter how she tried to discipline herself, to keep her mind on their quest, her thoughts kept wandering back to that beach, to the raw excitement generated between them. She wondered how much further things might have progressed had they been in a more appropriate setting.

Despite their differences, she was intrigued by Riley more than any man she'd ever known...and she couldn't possibly be hung up on a murderer. Her degree in psychology gave her some insights into human character, and she felt certain that while Riley O'Hare was quick to anger, he was no killer.

Even so, when he asked, "Anything else you've been keeping to yourself?" she couldn't bring herself to tell him.

Pulse throbbing unevenly, she hedged. "Like what?"

"Anybody else sneaking around the grounds? Anybody questioning you a little too closely."

"No."

At least that was the truth. Normally a very honest person, Marissa felt like a cheat. To her, omitting the truth was the same as lying. Again she rationalized that she couldn't let Riley know that she hadn't trusted him. If he probed any deeper, though, he would break her. Then everything would be out in the open between them.

But Riley chose that moment to fall into a thoughtful silence and concentrate on the water ahead.

And Marissa tried to find some relief in the fact that once more she was spared from revealing a secret that, if shared with the wrong person, could definitely get her killed.

"Do you think Mrs. Lynch will be able to tell us any more about Dori's big secret than what she already told Detective Lujan?" Marissa asked as they left the boat in the marina and headed out on foot for the nearby downtown area of Key West.

"Maybe the right questions will get us some answers that'll help us figure it out."

"Do you know her well?"

"Well enough." He was grimmer than usual. "I have to warn you, she doesn't like me much. Thought Dori could do better."

Lots of mothers felt that way about their daughters, so Marissa didn't think anything of it.

They entered an intriguing lane in what was known as Old Town. The street was decked out with beautiful homes, most more than a century old. Many of the buildings were large and covered with gingerbread—patterned with pineapples, fleurs-de-lis, urns and ship wheels. Natives of Key West were known as Conchs, and Conch architecture was considered the indigenous look of the island.

They approached one of the prettiest houses on the block. Its exterior walls painted violet, the two-story structure sat on piers—slabs of coral elevating the house against storms—and gingerbread-trimmed porches curved around three sides of both stories. Top-hung shutters kept the sun from intruding, and ventilating scuttles on the roof allowed the hot air to escape.

Riley cupped her elbow as they made their way up the steps, and it was he who clacked the fish-shaped door knocker against its wooden panel.

A moment later, the door was opened by a sober-looking woman in her late fifties or early sixties. She wore an old-fashioned mourning dress, plain gray with a neat, lace-trimmed collar, and bore a vague resemblance to Dori despite her graying hair and wire-rimmed eyeglasses.

The faded and watery blue eyes behind the thick lenses were filled with animosity as they lit on Riley. "What do you want? There's nothing for you here anymore." Her voice cracked on the last word.

"We need to talk to you, Viola," Riley said, his tone kind despite the woman's obvious dislike of him. "Can we please come in?"

Though she did so grudgingly, Mrs. Lynch stepped back without closing the door. The inside of her front parlor was as old-fashioned as the exterior of the house. She took her place in a rocking chair and indicated the ancient faded green sofa with spindly wooden legs. Hoping the thing wouldn't collapse under them, Marissa sat gingerly, Riley following suit.

The atmosphere between the other two tense, Marissa said, "Mrs. Lynch, I want you to know how sorry I am about your daughter."

The older woman squinted at her. "Do I know you?"

"I'm Marissa Gilmore from the Bal Harbour Oceanarium. I was the one who, uh, found Dori."

Instinctively pulling out a fancy handkerchief from a pocket, Mrs. Lynch clutched the square as she murmured, "Terrible, a terrible tragedy that my Dori died so young." Sniffling, she patted her nose with the lace-edged linen.

"Yes, it was," Marissa agreed. "Listen, Mrs. Lynch, we're not here to upset you. We hoped you might be able to help us find the man responsible for her death."

"I told the police everything I know."

"You mentioned something about a secret," Riley prompted.

Mrs. Lynch nodded. "The secret got Dori killed."

"What kind of secret?"

"Maybe you already know."

When he didn't respond but merely stared at her in tight-lipped silence, Marissa assured the older woman, "We don't know or we wouldn't be here."

"Not you. Him."

Viola Lynch never took her gaze off Riley. Behind the lenses, her eyes looked huge. And accusing.

"I don't have a clue."

"You know about the land, all right."

Marissa frowned. "What land?"

Before Mrs. Lynch could answer, Riley interrupted. "Unless we figure out who had a reason to murder Dori, Miss Gilmore here may be the next victim."

Viola appeared to be checking out the two of them. She visibly stiffened. "Is this your newest woman? Is she the one you threw my Dori over for?"

Marissa gave him a quick look. She hadn't heard anything about another woman, which certainly hadn't been her since they'd only just met.

"I didn't throw Dori over for anyone," Riley said. "The breakup was strictly between Dori and me. We had a major disagreement, and I realized we weren't right for each other."

Marissa got the feeling he was soft-soaping the breakup for Mrs. Lynch's benefit.

"You were right enough to get my girl pregnant!" the woman cried.

"*If* I was the father—"

"You calling my girl a trollop?" Viola Lynch's voice rose. "You think she would go with just anyone? No, you knew she was going to have your baby and broke it off. You should have done right by her!"

"I didn't even know about the baby until the medical examiner made his report."

Marissa started. All along she'd been comparing his irresponsibility toward Dori and his unborn child to her father's negligence toward her own family, but if Riley could be believed, he hadn't even known.

"She loved you and you broke her heart!"

"I never meant to break anyone's heart."

Aghast at the escalating argument—the woman had just lost her daughter, after all—and thinking to get the conversation back on track, Marissa intervened. "Mrs. Lynch, why is it you think this secret of Dori's got her killed?"

"'Cause she was all twisted up inside. Said she had to do something about it and that *he* would be furious with her." Again, the accusing stare at Riley.

"When was this?" Marissa asked.

"The day before she died. Dori came to see me unexpectedly. I knew something wasn't right. I asked her what was eating her. She didn't want to tell me straight out, but I got enough out of her to be worried."

"So she didn't say anything more specific than that she knew some secret about some land and that she had to do something about it?"

"That was it." Tears rolled down the distraught woman's cheeks. "If only she had been honest with me, maybe I could've helped her." She glared at Riley. "Maybe my girl wouldn't be dead now."

Someone once said the better part of valor was knowing when to be discreet. Marissa figured that time was now. Questioning the woman further would only deepen her wound and would get them no closer to the truth. Added to that, she feared Riley couldn't take much more of Viola Lynch's accusations and hostile looks before blowing up himself.

She rose. "Thank you for seeing us, Mrs. Lynch. And again, my condolences regarding Dori."

Riley's gaze locked with hers. Certain he wasn't ready to leave yet, Marissa refused to back down. She gave him a look that he couldn't misunderstand—she wanted out of there. Now.

Finally he rose.

"Viola," he mumbled, nodding politely as he followed Marissa outside.

Surprisingly, once they were on the sidewalk, he didn't give her a hard time about making the decision to leave. He merely said, "Let's walk over to Duval Street."

They strolled through a traffic jam of cars and motorcycles in an uneasy silence, Viola Lynch's final words echoing through her head.

If only she had been honest with me, maybe I could've helped her...maybe my girl wouldn't be dead now.

What if Mrs. Lynch had been correct? What if Dori's telling her mother everything she knew would have saved her life? What if *her* not telling someone about the scuba diver with the Predator equipment got her killed? Riley would be the logical person to tell. After all, he had come to her rescue three times now.

She was struggling with guilt as they walked down Duval. The street was crawling with tourists who frequented the various junky souvenir shops, tony art galleries, trendy restaurants and funky bars. A biker revved his motorcycle and progressed through the traffic jam by weaving around the crawling cars.

"Looks like we made the trip for nothing," Riley finally said, sounding disgusted. "We don't know anything more than we did before."

"We know this secret of Dori's has to do with land." Remembering how he'd cut off that line of questioning, she again asked, "But what land?"

"Viola wasn't specific."

Marissa had a strong feeling that Riley knew exactly what Viola Lynch had meant. "The refuge."

He glowered at her. "Drop it."

Control freak that he was, rudely cutting her off was Riley's only solution to avoiding whatever topic he didn't choose to discuss.

Not this time.

"I don't want to drop it!" she insisted. "If we're going to work this out together, then we need to be honest with each other." Both of them. That included her. Thinking that if she went first, he would follow suit, she bit the bullet. "For example, there's something that I've sort of neglected to tell you."

His eyebrows arched. "As in . . . ?"

Swallowing hard, Marissa said, "The night of the murder. I, uh, finally did remember something odd. When I was on the beach searching for Kamiko, someone ran out of the surf and into me. Literally."

"So someone was swimming at night."

"Not exactly. This person was wearing scuba gear," she said, wincing inside when his expression darkened. Playing true confessions was every bit as difficult as she'd feared it would be. "And when he ran into me, we fell to the sand and kind of hooked together. He was frantic to free himself and get away."

"He." His tone cool, Riley asked, "You're sure it was a man?"

She could hardly look him in the eye now. "No, not really. But if it was a woman, she was no lightweight. The person was pretty big." In for a penny... She took a deep breath. "And whoever it was left something behind... an object that may help us find the murderer. I found it stuck to my wet suit before I went diving yesterday."

"And what would that be?"

"A tiny metal shark. The kind identifying—"

"Predator equipment," he finished for her as they approached Mallory Square.

The mammoth crowd was peppered with street entertainers and vendors. Every other tourist had camera in hand. Over the gulf, the sun appeared to grow larger and more golden, sending out colorful streaks as it sank toward the horizon, a view that no tourist worth his salt would miss.

A romantic view for lovers.

Marissa shifted uneasily at the thought, especially since Riley was looking at her as if he'd tried, convicted and sentenced her.

"How long have you held back this information?" he asked as a juggler began showing off his skills nearby.

"Just since yesterday."

"Just?" His voice grew downright cold. "On the way here, didn't I ask if there was anything else you'd been keeping to yourself? And didn't you deny it?"

Growing defensive, she insisted, "I had my reasons." Like not wanting him to look at her as if she were something that had just crawled up out of some sewer, for one.

"I'm sure you did."

Face flaming, Marissa was now hesitant to demand that Riley tell her exactly what he thought he knew about Dori's secret—how the refuge might be involved in her death. So she turned her attention to a street entertainer, who was juggling at least five balls. Several people crowded between them to get a better look. Moving over to give them room, she was suddenly elbowed to one side. Off balance, she almost fell. A man caught her arm and steadied her.

"Thanks," she said. Even so, it took her a minute to regain her equilibrium—and to realize that she'd been separated from Riley. She forced her way back to where they'd been standing together, but he was gone!

Now what?

Fighting her way through the crowd, she searched for him, but the situation was impossible. Hundreds of people packed Mallory Square, and for some reason, she was spooked. They would never find each other here until the gathering thinned. But Riley hadn't said anything about staying late. Maybe when he didn't find her, he would head back to the boat, thinking she would do the same.

Reluctantly she broke through the throng and made off in the general direction of the marina, trying to negate her growing sense of unease.

Nothing to worry about, she told herself, as she bought a Miami paper from a newsstand. The headline about the suit Ocean Watch was bringing against Marathon Fisheries caught her eye. Folding the newspaper and tucking it under her arm, she turned down a side street free of pedestrians and moving cars. Probably everyone had gathered in the square for the entertainment. Still, the narrow lane had a lonely feel that she didn't exactly like.

Her footsteps echoed along the buildings and a chill whispered down her spine. Marissa wished she wasn't alone. She wished Riley was here, scowl and all. She wished she hadn't waited so long to tell him about the scuba diver.

Guilty. Guilty. Guilty.

Maybe she ought to apologize. She certainly couldn't tell him *why* she'd withheld the information, but she could say she was sorry that she had.

Trying to compose a little speech in her head, she wasn't aware of anything but putting one foot in front of the other until an engine revved up almost directly behind her. Startled, she turned to see a motorcycle, its rider in jeans, black jacket and helmet, dark visor pulled over his face.

The hair rose on the back of her neck. . . .

Telling herself she was nuts, that she was reacting to nothing but her own imagination, she walked faster, anyway. But not fast enough to keep ahead of the motorcycle. She threw another glance over her shoulder and realized the rider was staring at her through the visor.

Then, with an ominous roar, the cycle leapt onto the sidewalk and headed straight for her.

Chapter Nine

Marissa blinked disbelievingly ... and ran for her life!

Behind her, the motorcycle's thunderous noise drew closer, nearly blotting out her thoughts. On instinct, even as she imagined the metallic beast's breath growing hot on her heels, she flew off the sidewalk and up a set of steps.

Her pursuer zoomed past, down the street, and shot around the corner.

Marissa's heart pounded as she watched the tail of the cycle disappear. She'd been certain the killer had somehow found her and had chosen to finish the job right here. Run over by a motorcycle—who would suspect anything more dastardly than a freak accident? But she'd been wrong. Undoubtedly the rider had been some creep who got his thrills by scaring unsuspecting victims.

"Hey, lady, you want something or what?" A wizened elderly man poked his head out his front door and glared at her through rheumy eyes.

Realizing she was on his steps, one hand curled into a tight fist around his railing, the other smashing the newspaper to her breast, she flushed and backed down. "No, nothing. Sorry. Wrong house."

As fast as her shaky knees would carry her, Marissa flew from the site. With trepidation, she made straight for the corner, keeping her eyes open.

No motorcycle, thank heavens.

Once across the street, she took a deep breath and continued walking briskly. She was only about two blocks from the marina; she'd be there in five minutes or so. A panic attack could wait until she was back on the refuge's boat.

Or so she thought.

For, halfway down the second block, Marissa heard it—the motorcycle engine revving up menacingly. Nothing behind her. Nothing ahead. The sound grew louder, causing her mouth to dry and her pulse to renew its furious beat. She hurried along, the engine's clamor echoing all around her, bouncing off the very buildings.

Suddenly a dark blur streaked out from between two low shotgun houses.

Marissa froze as the deadly-looking machine and rider came at her on the sidewalk again. If she stood there, she wouldn't live to tell the tale, but she couldn't outrun the damn thing. Her mind worked quickly, her occupied hand following instinctively. Unfurling the newspaper, she flung it directly at the rider and dodged into the street at the same time. The cyclist tried to follow, but a gust of wind tossed the large sheets of paper into the air and the fluttering pages spread and plastered themselves to her pursuer's chest and face.

The cycle went out of control even as Marissa ran past it, continuing in the direction of the marina. The sound of a crash behind her and a loud yelp made her take a quick look back. Engine dead, the cycle had skidded down the street on its side, having left its rider behind in the dirt.

Elated, Marissa ran for all she was worth, not glancing back until she got to the next corner. Her pursuer was on his feet, examining his leg. She sped across the street and checked again. He was picking up his bike. Terror shot through her again. Her lungs burned and her legs ached from the effort of running.

A cautious look told her the rider was back in the saddle, but the motorcycle's engine didn't seem to be starting.

Only then, when she realized he didn't have the means to chase after her, did Marissa dare slow her pace. A moment later, she stumbled into the last intersection and recklessly dodged cars on the busy street. Once across, she stopped and scrutinized the area for her pursuer.

All was clear. Puffing and staggering, she made her way to the marina and to the pier where they had docked. Standing near a luxury yacht, a pair of men broke off their conversation to turn and stare at her as she passed.

"Riley!" she gasped as she drew closer to the refuge boat.

She might as well have saved her breath, for she received no answer. Other than its creaking as it dipped and swayed with the current, the boat remained silent. Exhausted, her legs wobbly, she lunged over the side and dropped down onto the deck, where she allowed herself to collapse.

Huddled against the outside of the cabin wall, she recouped her equilibrium. Decided she would live. And waited for Riley's return. Where the hell was he? What if the killer came looking for her here? A good half hour passed before she heard uneven footsteps moving down the pier.

Forcing herself to her feet, she watched Riley come toward the boat, his expression grim.

He was *limping* . . . as if he'd had an accident.

A motorcycle accident?

Heart in her throat, she watched Riley jump over the side of the boat onto the deck, wincing as he touched down, and wondered if she hadn't taken shelter in the one place that wasn't in the least bit safe.

"What's wrong with your leg?" Marissa asked, a knot in her stomach.

"Slight accident. Some woman in the crowd ran square into my shin with one of those huge baby strollers. Nearly knocked me over. I saw stars."

A likely story . . . one she should believe?

"When I regained my balance, you'd vanished." Riley took a good look at her and frowned. "What happened to you?"

Marissa pushed at the strands of escaped hair around her face, but there was nothing she could do about her strained expression. Or her voice. Tightly she said, "Someone tried running me over with a motorcycle."

You? she wanted to ask.

He shook his head. "You've got to be careful. Damn tourists don't watch where they're going."

"This was no tourist."

"How do you know?"

"A tourist wouldn't have any reason to try a second time."

His face seemed wreathed in a dark thundercloud as her statement sank in. "You're telling me someone deliberately tried running you down?"

"That's the ticket." Marissa's stomach relaxed a bit when he truly seemed surprised.

Riley spun around and he quickly scanned their surroundings. "How long ago did this happen?"

"Long enough. Can we get out of here?"

He nodded. "Good idea."

They untied the lines and Riley took the helm. Marissa lingered at the rail, staring out toward the street, hoping to catch a glimpse of a visored, black-jacketed man on a motorcycle. Seeing him while Riley was here with her would prove that Riley couldn't be the one.

No such luck.

They set off for Lime Key, and with her whole heart, Marissa wished she could put a damper on her persistent suspicions and give Riley O'Hare her complete trust.

The boat trip back was made in complete silence, as she was lost in speculation.

THE EARLY MORNING HOURS denied Marissa sleep. Not that she'd had much, anyway. She'd spent the night tossing and turning between sweet dreams and nightmares, all of which featured Riley. To her dismay, she was becoming so obsessed with the man, she couldn't even escape him in slumber.

Though dawn was still a few minutes away, she rose and dressed. Her mind was spinning with all that had happened to her in the past week. Someone was out to kill her, and the only clues she had were a tiny metal shark, a note to Dori in an elegant handwriting and Mrs. Lynch's vague reference to land being the secret that got her daughter killed.

Maybe a walk would help make things clearer for her.

Through the stand of palms surrounding her cabin, pale pink streaked the gray sky to the east, heralding the arrival of the sun. She automatically headed in the opposite direction, along the path leading toward the refuge, not expecting to hear voices coming from the property at this hour.

"What's done is done," came a voice she easily recognized. "Can't go back and change it. Dori's dead and that's that."

Erasmus North! And he was talking about the murder! Pulse charging with that knowledge, Marissa sneaked forward and stopped behind a grove of palm trees near the food-preparation building, as Erasmus followed Riley's housekeeper outside. They started on the path back to the house.

Billie was saying, "Dori'd still be alive if she'd left well enough alone."

"I can't keep good enough tabs on Riley, what with him gallivanting around like he's been doing this past week," the fisherman complained.

"You'd best be careful," Billie warned him, her voice fading with distance. "If Riley ever finds out who you are, the game'll be up."

Marissa couldn't hear any more without openly following them and risking their seeing her. So, Erasmus and Billie were in cahoots. About what? Dori's murder? Who exactly was Erasmus, and what game was he playing?

Was there anyone on the island she shouldn't be suspicious of?

Maybe Luke. And Ken, she conceded, waiting until she was certain she was alone before breaking cover and heading for the pens.

Sitting down on the boardwalk, she spent the next hour watching Kamiko interact with her new companions. The three females were getting along like old friends. Kamiko was even showing interest in the calf. While Marissa had hoped the transition would be as smooth as possible for the dolphin, she hadn't expected Kamiko to adapt quite this fast. From the way things were progressing, she wouldn't really be needed here much longer. She could probably go home soon. Tomorrow, even.

That should make her happy... so why didn't it?

Once she left Lime Key, she wouldn't be able to help search for Dori's killer, Marissa told herself. A depressing thought. The murderer wasn't about to give up on *her.* She would have to sit and wait, fearful that he'd catch up to her before someone else caught him.

That had to be what was disturbing her.

She couldn't be depressed because she might never see Riley again. Could she?

The truth niggled at her until Marissa had to face it. She didn't want to be without Riley. She'd gotten used to his glowering and his creepy way of sneaking up on her...not to mention his being there when she needed him.

Needed him. That held an ominous ring for a woman who'd been a free spirit her whole adult life. Especially since she wasn't one hundred percent sure of him.

But doubting Riley was ridiculous. If he'd wanted her dead, why had he bothered to open the freezer door? And there had been no witnesses out in Florida

Bay. If he'd cut the line to the skiff and had been hanging around to make sure she was dead, why had he rescued her and brought her back to the refuge? He could so easily have left her to drown, a real possibility, especially considering the storm.

She had to operate on the premise that Riley was innocent. That he was on her side even if he wasn't very open and on the up-and-up about everything. He was hiding something that had to do with the refuge, or else he wouldn't have cut her off when she asked him to explain Mrs. Lynch's statement about the land. But whatever he was holding back from her couldn't have anything to do with Dori's death—she had to believe that.

Convincing herself made Marissa feel better. Thinking about leaving the refuge didn't. Then again, Paul had entrusted the decision about when to return to Bal Harbour Oceanarium to her own discretion. A smile slowly curled her lips as she thought about that. She'd leave when she was good and ready, when she and Riley had caught the bastard who'd killed Dori and was now trying to rid himself of her, too.

That resolution made, Marissa realized she was hungry and set off for the house, wondering when she could get Riley alone to tell him about Billie and Erasmus, so they could discuss how to proceed.

By the time she arrived at the deck, Riley was already eating with his son.

"I took a look at the budget and figured we could squeeze enough money out of it for supplies to install that underwater gate for Brutus," Riley was telling Luke as she approached the buffet table and filled a mug with coffee.

"Yeah?"

"I thought we could work on it together. If you're interested."

"Of course I'm interested. I've got some other ideas for the refuge, too, uh, if you want to hear them, that is."

"I'd like that, son."

Filling her plate with bacon and scrambled eggs, Marissa was warmed as she listened. Maybe Riley wasn't like her father, after all. He'd claimed not to have known about Dori's pregnancy, and now here he was, really trying to get closer to Luke. So maybe *his* dream wasn't more important than the people in his life.

About to take a seat at another table, she hesitated when Riley said, "Marissa, is there some reason you want to eat alone this morning?"

She looked at Luke, remembering his reaction when he'd found her and Riley in each other's arms.

As if he remembered, too, the teenager reddened. "Uh, we've got room. You can sit here."

"Great." Getting herself settled, she said, "Installing that gate for Brutus will make your lives a lot easier. Too bad you can't figure out a way to keep him away from Toby Hanson's property when he does get out."

"Mr. Hanson doesn't own the water," Luke groused.

"He thinks he does." Riley took a big slug of coffee. "He'd like to own the whole island if he could."

Munching on a piece of bacon, Marissa said, "Vida told me he wanted to buy the refuge. You wouldn't consider selling, would you?"

"Never."

"Dad can't, 'cause he doesn't own the property."

Riley quickly cut in, "Yet," and gave his son a warning look.

Luke renewed his interest in his breakfast, shoveling a forkful of eggs into his mouth.

But Marissa refused to let the subject go. She pinned Riley with her gaze. "So you're what—leasing the land with the intention to buy?"

"Something like that."

"If we ever get the money," Luke grumbled.

Marissa offered, "I could make some suggestions on how to do that."

Riley's tone went flat. "I'm sure."

"What kind of suggestions?" Luke asked, chancing another dark look from his father.

"More tours, for one. Plus, other refuges have educational programs for tourists—"

Riley cut her off. "I suppose you want me to let people whom I know nothing about swim with the dolphins."

"Why not? Swim programs bring in vital money— you just need to make the cost of participating high enough, so that you exclude all those who just want to make mischief. And you can't beat the public relations aspect, either. People go away from swim programs in love with the dolphins and concerned about their welfare. And extra donations aren't unheard of."

"No."

"No?" A wide-eyed Marissa stared at him. "Just like that?"

"No," Riley repeated.

"You won't even consider doing something that would allow you to upgrade the place—not to mention making enough money so you can think about buying the land?"

"No!" This was final. Pushing away from the table, Riley picked up his plate, which was still half-full, and then thought better of it and set it back down. "I've got to check on Anook." And he left abruptly, almost running into Vida and Ken.

Subdued by his volatile reaction, Marissa barely touched the rest of her breakfast and was torn about getting back to work. On the one hand, she would be close to Riley; on the other, she would be close to Riley.

How could he thrill her one moment and put her off so completely the next? Startled by the unexpected answer that popped into her mind, Marissa tried to deny it. While her body definitely had an interest in Riley's, she couldn't possibly be falling in love with the man himself....

BUT THE AGGRAVATING notion of possibly being in love wouldn't go away. It bothered Marissa all day, making her reluctant to spend any time alone with Riley. Though alone they must be in order to discuss continuing their investigation. Marissa told herself she would just have to keep her emotions in tight check.

She found her opportunity to talk to him in private late that afternoon, when Luke and Vida and Ken dispersed to take care of other tasks on the refuge. She and Riley were left to weigh out dolphin chow together. Entering the food-prep building still gave her the heebie-jeebies. She hadn't been inside more than a minute or two since being locked in the freezer.

Merely being near Riley in an enclosed space put her senses on alert. She couldn't help herself. Her heart thumped, her breath grew shallow, her head felt a little light. And then he opened the freezer. The metallic creak of hinges got an even greater reaction out of her. She took a good look at the door when he swung it open.

"It's fixed."

"So to speak."

While a new release handle was rigged in place, and some of the splintered wood had been removed, there was still a ragged hole.

"Luckily I'm pretty handy." Riley disappeared inside the freezer and seconds later carried out a tray of frozen fish. "I told anyone who was interested that I accidentally locked myself inside."

She couldn't stop herself from shuddering at the thought. "And they believed you?"

He nodded. "All but the one person who knows better, of course."

That reminded her of the fisherman sneaking around the property that night and led her to the subject she wanted most to discuss. "How well do you know Erasmus North, other than the fact he delivers fish to the refuge every morning?" she asked, filling and weighing the first bucket. Concentrating on trying to finger a murderer, she could almost ignore the invisible pull between them as they worked shoulder-to-shoulder.

"Over the years, Erasmus and I have probably had a few dozen beers together, during which time we've discussed politics, philosophy and other various subjects."

His voice was mellifluous, the same smooth tone he'd used the first night she'd met him, and Marissa realized he felt the pull, too. Their eyes met and she stood gaping at him for a moment, before remembering her purpose.

"Do you know where he lives?" she asked a bit breathlessly, forcing herself to start on the next bucket. "Who his friends are?"

"Why the questions?"

"Do you?"

"He's got a place over on Marathon," Riley said, referring to one of the Middle Keys. Grabbing several other buckets, he set them out on the counter. "Been there a couple of times. As for his friends..." He shook his head. "Other than a bar buddy or two, I wouldn't know."

Marissa took a big breath and quickly related the snatch of dialogue she'd overheard between Erasmus and Billie that morning—the two of them discussing Dori's death, the fisherman making a reference to his following Riley, the housekeeper indicating Riley didn't know who Erasmus was, and that if he did, the game would be up.

"Hell!" Riley's hands clenched one of the buckets. "They couldn't be involved...they couldn't. Not Billie."

Uneasiness crept through Marissa. He almost sounded like he knew who *was* involved. That he refused to consider Wilhemina Van Zandt might be suspect, as well. Surely he wouldn't choose to be blind if they found proof. She could only hope he wasn't keeping anything important from her.

"Billie hated Dori," she told him, uncertain if he knew.

"Hate's a strong word. Did Billie tell you that?"

"Not exactly. But she didn't leave any doubt in my mind that you're like a son to her and she thought Dori was only out to take you." That was when it hit her. Riley didn't even own the refuge—so what kind of material gain *had* Billie thought Dori was after?

"Those feelings don't mean she would do anything to harm Dori," Riley argued.

"What if she got Erasmus to do the dirty work? The two of them seem pretty close, in case you haven't noticed."

While she was trying to imagine either the house-keeper or the fisherman being the scuba diver who'd run into her on the beach that fateful night, Riley silently grabbed clumps of frozen fish and threw them into buckets.

"Or maybe it was Erasmus's idea," she went on, more to herself than to him. The housekeeper wasn't big enough, she decided, but the fisherman could have been the one. "Billie said that if you found out who Erasmus was, the game would be up. So, other than a fisherman, who exactly could he be?"

"I don't know, but I intend to find out."

"You're not going to confront him."

"Why shouldn't I?"

"Because if he's guilty, then you'll be a target, too," Marissa said, not adding that if the murderer felt threatened, he might kill first, think later. The idea of Riley dead left a hole in her heart, and she knew it was too late to keep her emotions in control. "Better to hold the questions until we have something more substantial."

"Like what?"

"Like finding out who wrote Dori that note."

"Whoever wrote it isn't necessarily guilty of murder."

Riley had said the handwriting looked like a woman's. Billie's? If so, he didn't seem anxious to admit it.

So she changed tactics. "True. But something was obviously going on. Maybe the note can lead us to some specific fact that would be of help. Like...what about the cabin where they were to meet?"

"The author wasn't specific."

"No, but if they were going to meet in private...this isn't a very big island." Marissa stopped work for a moment. "How many cabins are there?"

"In addition to the refuge, there's the resort, Hanson's place and two small vacation homes on the other side of the island. Both of those have been in use for months, and there are no cabins or bungalows or guest houses of any kind on Hanson's property."

"That leaves the refuge or the resort."

"We've got three bungalows in the refuge. Dori's, Vida's and Ken's."

Riley was working on automatic pilot, and Marissa noticed he'd filled the buckets with far too many fish. The dolphins were going to pig out unless he stopped now. Aware of his simmering emotions—because she'd dared to implicate Billie?—she decided this was not the moment to correct him.

"The person didn't say 'meet me at your place' or 'meet me at my place,'" she said. "The resort is it then. But how do we figure out which of the dozen cabins—"

"Some are empty. Lime Tree Resort is rarely full at this time of the year."

"So if I can find out which cabins have been empty for the past several weeks..."

Riley plopped two of the overfilled buckets near the door. "What do you mean—find out?"

"I'm on a first-name basis with the owner."

"Stay away from Roche." His tone left no room for doubt that he was giving her an order.

Meeting his glowering expression with one of her own, she said, "I beg your pardon?"

"He's a parasite. He preys on lonely women."

Suddenly Riley looked as if he wanted to prey on *her*. Though her mouth went dry and her speeding pulse made her anxious, Marissa refused to give ground, physically or verbally. The control freak needed to know he didn't have all the answers, that she was an independent woman who could make her own decisions.

"I never said I was lonely. And I *will* talk to him. Tonight at dinner."

"I don't like it."

She said, "No one asked you," as he moved in on her.

Marissa sensed his repressed aggression. Even as she yearned to have his arms around her, she wouldn't allow it, not like this, not when he had something to prove. Like his mastery over her.

So when he reached out a hand to pull her toward him, she smacked it away and jerked back against the counter. "Don't!"

His expression grim, he advanced on her, his very nearness making her body respond. "Why not?"

"Because I said not to." She held out her arm to halt his advance and then quickly ducked out of his way. "You can't order me to stay away from Roche, and you can't seduce me into doing what you want, either."

That stopped him cold. An indefinable expression passed over his features—almost as if he was confused. Riley O'Hare confused? More like cunning,

Marissa assured herself, steeling herself for the next attack.

"Can I ask you to be careful?"

She blinked, amazed that he'd made a one-hundred-and-eighty-degree turn so fast. "That would be kind of nice." She couldn't help wondering whether or not she should be suspicious.

But she was tired of distrusting Riley. If he had secrets, he had good cause, she assured herself. He really was looking out for her best interests, no matter how badly he might handle himself at times.

"Then please be careful." Without touching her, Riley reached around and picked up two more buckets, frowning when the burden jerked his arms down hard. "Damn! We forgot to weigh these."

Marissa smothered the grin that threatened to escape her.

They spent the next few minutes rectifying the situation. Too aware of Riley for comfort, Marissa remedied that by occupying her mind elsewhere, plotting how she would get the information she needed from Ansel Roche.

IF ONLY ANSEL WERE available when Marissa thought to put her plan into action . . .

The owner of Lime Tree Resort was sitting at a table with two men she'd never seen before—one thin and dark and weathered, the other burly and fair and young. New guests? If so, they needed to relax and get rid of the suits.

She slipped onto a stool at the bar and ordered a piña colada. The mirror in back of the bar gave her a perfect view of the three men. Anxiously she waited for Ansel to leave the table. She'd counted on his seeking her out for a friendly word or two as he did every night. Tonight, he didn't seem to be aware that she existed.

Nor did the two people at the table in the farthest corner of the room. Cole Glaser...and Vida Dalberg. Glaser covered one of Vida's hands with his own, and he was leaning closer than would be acceptable if they were merely acquaintances. Vida was smiling at the sandy-haired man. It looked as if the two had something going.

A flash of Riley pinning Glaser to a tree came to mind. Riley had been threatening the smaller man. To stay away from Vida?

No sooner had the question posed itself than movement at a closer table caught her attention. The two strangers and Ansel were standing. Leaving. All of them. Her stomach sank as she saw her plan fall apart.

Via the mirror, she watched them leave the restaurant. Once they were outside, she observed them more directly through the big screened wall. They went straight for the dock and the luxury craft berthed there. Ansel and the weathered-looking man shook hands, while the young, burly one stood back, hands folded in front of him, seemingly at attention...as if on the alert. How odd.

The older guy must be some rich friend of Ansel's; the young one his bodyguard. Whoever they were didn't matter. They were leaving. And Ansel wasn't.

Realizing she hadn't touched her drink, Marissa picked it up and moved to a table near the door. A moment later, the owner of Lime Tree Resort walked in, and though he looked straight at her, he didn't seem to see her. His expression was closed. Worried. No, more like disgruntled.

"Ansel, good evening," Marissa said loudly enough that he couldn't overlook her.

Finally he recognized her presence. A smooth smile stretching his lips, Ansel came straight to her table as if he'd meant to all along.

"How nice to see you, Marissa." As if he didn't see her every night. "My favorite guest."

"If that's true, then why don't you join me for dinner?"

"Done." With something of a smug smile, he slid into the seat opposite.

"I dragged you home so early the other night, we hardly had a chance to get acquainted."

"I'm flattered."

Ansel lifted her hand and touched his lips to her knuckles. *Uh-oh.* She wanted information, not to give him any ideas. Though, in fact, she wasn't sure that he was actually coming on to her. More like he was practicing.

Gently removing her hand from his, she said, "There are so few people on the island that it would be nice to get to know them all."

He didn't so much as blink, but merely said, "Of course." He smiled, his teeth white against his deep tan. "And who wouldn't be honored to know such a charming young woman as yourself."

With his smooth good looks and smooth line, Ansel could be quite charming. She wondered if Riley's accusations of Ansel's being a parasite had equal credence with Ansel's saying Riley used women and broke their hearts. She, of course, hoped Ansel was wrong about Riley. For some reason, the men didn't like each other, and she couldn't possibly make judgments about which one of them—if either—was correct.

After they placed their orders, she let Ansel lead the conversation for a few minutes, answering questions about her work and background. Perfect, since she planned to ask him about his business. Her opportunity came when the waiter interrupted with their first course.

A few seconds later, she casually said, "Say, I saw those two men leaving earlier. Business must be great if you're turning away new guests."

"Hardly. They were business acquaintances."

"So the resort is what?" She looked around at the tables in use and noticed that Cole Glaser and Vida had left. "Half-full?"

"About."

"What a shame more people don't know what a paradise this place is, even in the off-season." This was it. Pulse throbbing, hoping he wouldn't clam up or change the subject, she asked, "So what do you do— lock up some of the cabins for the whole summer to save on maintenance costs?"

"Actually, we do extra upkeep during the off-season," Ansel told her. "A couple of the cabins are undergoing some minor renovations, so they won't be back in use until the work is finished, which had better be in time for the Memorial Day weekend since I've already booked them."

Marissa smiled. He'd told her what she needed to know. Her mind was only half on their conversation throughout the rest of the meal, but if Ansel noticed, he didn't indicate as much.

When they'd finished, he refused to let her sign the bill, insisting that dinner was on him. "Next time, I'll take you to my favorite supper club over in Islamorada."

Knowing she wouldn't be going anywhere with him, Marissa smiled and rose. "You're too generous."

"Not at all." He stood, too, and took her hand. "I only wish you were going to be a permanent member of the refuge staff. Lime Key could use some delicious new blood."

She was relieved to escape his oozing charm.

Rather than going straight back to her quarters, she changed her route in order to find the empty cabins. Stone paths crisscrossed throughout the junglelike garden area. Approaching one unit, she could barely make out the next closest one. The place certainly was meant for privacy and a sure bet for Dori and the mysterious author of the note to have a secret meeting.

The first few cabins were lit up and obviously in use. The next one was empty, but if it was being worked on, she couldn't tell.

Midway through her exploration, she hesitated, alarmed by a soft *shoosh* somewhere in the vicinity. Holding her breath, she stepped through some bushes, away from the soft light along the path, and into the shelter of a large palm tree. Frozen there, she waited and listened, but the sound wasn't repeated. Nor did she catch sight of any movement. Undoubtedly she'd heard some small animal scurrying along the ground.

Remembering the coral snake, Marissa shuddered and immediately tried to inspect the ground around her feet. But away from the path, it was too dark to see a thing.

Cautiously she stepped back onto the stone walkway and continued her exploration, stopping every so often to scan the various paths crossing around her. Though she never spotted anyone, never heard another sound, she couldn't shake the feeling that she wasn't alone.

By the time she'd made the rounds and reached her place, she'd spotted five empty cabins, three of which were in various stages of renovation. Exploring vague notions of somehow getting into those cabins and searching them, she remained distracted until she heard a crunch in the undergrowth behind her. Her pulse immediately trip-hammered, and she was trying to decide if she'd be foolish or brave to face whoever was following her, when the decision was made for her.

A hand gripped her upper arm and spun her around.

Marissa barely swallowed a scream.

Chapter Ten

"Riley O'Hare, either you're going to give me a heart attack, or I'm going to flatten you if you keep this up!" Marissa's heart thundered as she irately stared at his maddeningly neutral expression. She was tempted to punch him—she really was. He certainly was close enough to touch. She stepped back, out of range of his personal radar before the temptation grew. "How dare you follow me!"

"I've been waiting for you right here for nearly half an hour." Neutrality suddenly became disapproval. "Enjoy your dinner with Roche?"

Her eyebrows shot up. "As a matter of fact, I did. The resort's food is delicious."

"And the man?"

Marissa ignored that and turned toward her door. Surely he couldn't be jealous—though she wasn't certain she would mind if he was. Thinking about the possibility gave her a little thrill she couldn't deny. "Let's go inside."

So she hadn't been followed, after all. Or had she? Some instinct wouldn't allow her to let go of the idea.

"So what's the skinny?" Riley demanded before he even got both feet over the threshold.

Marissa waited until he closed the door behind him. "The scoop is that three of the guest quarters haven't been rented out for several weeks because they're being renovated," she said triumphantly.

"That's it?"

"Isn't that enough? What else did you expect?" Before he could answer, she said, "Well, actually, I found them, as well. There's the cabin in back of this one, and the other two are on the east side of the resort. Now if only we could figure out how to get inside..."

"So what's the problem?"

Their gazes connected and she realized he meant to break in, if necessary. That led her to wondering if he'd done this kind of thing before, but she couldn't bring herself to ask about his previous experience.

They left immediately, Marissa peering around warily just to be on the safe side. The tiniest unease in the pit of her stomach made her want to be doubly careful that they worked unobserved. The sound she'd heard earlier must still be spooking her, because if anything larger than a rodent lurked nearby, surely she would have seen some sign.

The cabin nearest hers was right in the middle of a face-lift. The door was unlocked and the windows had been left open, but the room still reeked of fresh paint.

She flicked on the light. If the place had been used for Dori's rendezvous with the author of the note, Marissa certainly couldn't tell. The furniture and floors were shrouded with covers. A ladder was still set up in the kitchen area where cabinet doors had been removed and new tile had been laid. Paint cans and half-empty bags of plaster and grout sat in one corner.

"From the looks of it, I doubt we've got the right place. This kind of work isn't done overnight," Riley pronounced, "or even in a week."

"The other two cabins are more isolated, anyway," Marissa said, hoping they wouldn't find them in the same condition. "Either of them would be a better bet."

Shutting off the light and taking care to close the door so no one would know they'd been there, she led the way to the second building. Every so often she looked over her shoulder, half-expecting to see a dark shadow moving out from the shelter of a palm tree.

Nothing, of course. She was merely on edge.

While the door of the next cabin was locked, the windows were still left opened because of the paint smell, making entry a snap, thank goodness. Riley lifted a sash, climbed inside and held out a hand to her.

When she took it, Marissa was thrilled by his touch as always, and much more so after softly falling against him the second her feet touched the floor. Riley's arms immediately circled around her back, steadying her. His breath fanned her face and she wondered what he intended.

A flare of desire warred with her determination to play detective, but in the end, she pushed herself away from him, telling herself it was for her own good.

She imagined his burning look through the dark, but then he hit the light switch next to the door. "Paint's still fresh," he commented as if unaffected by their intimate encounter.

She took a deep breath. "Not a sign of workmen in here."

And not a thing out of place. Though covered with a light coating of dust, the furniture looked undisturbed. Each piece seemed to have been precisely set for effect, as though the room was waiting for its Memorial Day occupants. Even the carpeting hadn't been walked on since the patterns of the vacuum cleaner were evident in the nap.

"Not a sign of any life," Marissa added, wandering around, poking into drawers and cabinets.

Still, they thoroughly checked the place out before choosing to go on to the cabin next door...which, unfortunately, was locked up tight.

"Now what?" she muttered.

"Time to check my credit."

"Huh?"

Wallet in hand, he pulled out a charge card. "Allow me." Gripping the knob, he inserted the plastic between door and jamb and carefully eased it downward. The responding *click* echoed clearly in the quiet of the night. "Didn't think it would be bolted since it's officially unoccupied."

Once more, Marissa goosenecked around to make certain no one had seen or heard them. No one, as far as she could tell.

She shook away the uneasy feeling that prying eyes were watching their every move. Once inside, door closed behind them, the soft golden light dispelled the remaining shadows in her mind.

Riley made a sound of disappointment. "Looks pretty much the same as the last cabin."

"No, not exactly," Marissa countered. "Someone's been in here since the renovation was finished." She pointed out the table and the dresser. "See, what dust there is has been disturbed." Glancing down, she said, "And we're not the first to walk on this carpeting since it's been vacuumed, either."

"Now if only we could get a clear footprint..." Riley said.

Frowning at the ridiculous idea of trying to get a print from a carpet, she met Riley's gaze. His expression was neutral, but laughter lurked in his green eyes. He was joking, something that was usually anathema to him. An answering smile hovered around her lips. If her hormones hadn't been interested before, they wouldn't be able to resist now.

"You should do that more often," she told him.

"What? Make facetious remarks?"

"Why not? It proves you're human."

"Was there ever any doubt?"

"You do have a reputation." Marissa remembered being prepared to dislike him, and, indeed, despite her attraction to the man, she'd seemed determined to do so. "I was warned before I ever set foot on Dolphin Haven soil."

Raising his eyebrows, he allowed his gaze to slip down her bare legs to her sandals. "And a very nice foot it is."

Cursing her tendency to flush, Marissa said, "We weren't talking about me."

"We weren't?" He widened his eyes. "Oh, that's right. We're here to search the place."

She swore he was smiling as he turned his back on her. Part of her speculated on his unusual mood, while another part pushed her into getting busy. She started with the dresser while he sauntered over to the closet. Anticipation grew in her with the opening of each drawer, but in the end she was disappointed.

Nothing.

"Find anything?" she asked, turning to discover him standing in the closet doorway, frozen and staring at something in his hands. "What?"

Coming up beside him, she saw the item that had him mesmerized. A lavender silk-and-lace teddy.

His voice hoarse, Riley said, "I found this at the back of the shelf."

"Maybe the last guest forgot it, and the painters skipped the closet." Even as she said it, Marissa knew there was something significant about the dainty lingerie.

"It belonged to Dori."

Because he should know, she didn't doubt him. "Then we've found the right place."

"She was meeting a man here."

He said the words calmly, but Marissa sensed he was holding himself in check. He was right, of course. No other reason for such a personal garment to be found in the cabin.

"Let's keep looking," she suggested, troubled by his reaction. She'd thought he was over Dori. Thought he had little more than contempt for the dead woman. Now she was thinking she'd been wrong. "Maybe we'll find something else."

Heading for the bathroom, she glanced over her shoulder. Riley was still standing there, staring down at the teddy. He deserved a moment alone to get his emotions under control. Though they weren't clear, they were potent enough to touch her across the room.

Anger or heartache—she might never know which.

Her search of the bathroom was purposeful. And slow. She didn't want to face Riley until he was his own surly self. When she thought he'd had enough time to pull himself together, she exited. "Nothing in there." She was relieved to find him in the kitchen area, running a hand along the shelf in a cabinet. She opened the refrigerator.

"I already checked that," he said flatly.

She closed it.

His back to her, Riley crossed to the sitting area and threw himself into the lone chair. So he wouldn't have to sit next to her? Aware of the grim line of his mouth, Marissa accommodated him and took the sofa.

"So how bad is it?" she dared to ask while trying to get comfortable. The cushions behind her didn't seem to be plumped up properly.

"Bad?" he echoed.

"The jealousy."

He grimaced and shook his head in denial. "You've got it all wrong."

"I don't think so."

How could he deny he was upset finding proof of Dori's faithlessness when it was clear in the tense line of his body, in his contorted expression? But then ... was it faithlessness if Riley had already broken up with Dori? Or could it be he'd just said that in order to save face when Dori had actually broken off with him?

Nearly convinced he still had a thing for the dead woman, Marissa was startled when Riley said, "I, uh, was pretty certain the baby was mine. Now I'm not sure who might responsible for Dori's pregnancy."

"Does it matter?"

"Of course it matters. I've been giving myself grief over the fact that I didn't know. That I would be robbed of being a father to my child all over again."

Riley sounded so serious that Marissa had to believe him. More of her doubts about his being committed to people who mattered slipped away....

She shifted and tried again to find a more comfortable position, but something was sticking her in the butt. "What the heck?" Reaching behind her, she plunged her hand down into the space between the cushions and grasped something hard and thin. She pulled it out. "An address book." She looked at Riley. "Dori's?"

He shrugged.

She flipped back the red leather cover. "No ID." After quickly taking stock of the handwriting—it was cramped and closed—she determined it was the exact opposite of the script they'd found in the note they'd found.

"That could've belonged to anyone," Riley was saying.

"Or not." Something told her to hang on to the thing. Just as something told her to get out while the going was good. She rose. "Let's take a better look at it at my place." When he didn't respond, she made up his mind for him, crossing to the door and switching off the light. "You'd better get a move on unless you want to sit there in the dark by yourself... alone with your memories."

The fact that he might desire that disturbed her. She was getting far too emotionally involved and had to either stop it or be sorely disappointed.

Then Riley rose and crossed the room, a silent, almost threatening, silhouette in the dark. As he drew closer, she couldn't help her automatic response to him. She wanted to wrap her arms around him and lay her cheek against his shoulder, but she slipped through the door instead, wincing at the sharp *click* as the wooden panel closed behind them.

They proceeded along the stone pathway in silence, Marissa more aware of Riley than of any possible physical danger. When they finally reached her cabin and entered the lit room, she sighed with relief—as if the familiar surroundings could protect her from herself.

Remembering the address book, she used it as a shield against her emotions, so that she wouldn't have to think about being hung up on a man who might be pining for someone he could never have. Pacing, she riffled through the pages, while he wedged a hip against the back of the couch.

"Actually, you should be the one looking for familiar names," she said, scanning the disappointingly few entries. All were foreign to her.

"Not necessarily. I didn't know any of Dori's friends outside of the marine mammal community."

Why didn't that surprise her?

Reaching the end of the address book, she noted there were no entries under *XYZ*. But on the inside of the last page—a blank—were two series of numbers lightly penciled in.

"Look. This one's obviously a phone number," she said, stopping at Riley's side and tapping a finger near the first set of digits. "But whose?"

Riley shook his head. "Don't recognize it."

"And what about this one?" She pointed to the four digits directly under the first series—eight-five-four-seven.

"Probably another extension that goes with the prefix. A fax machine?"

That sounded reasonable. "But why put it here in the back instead of under a letter corresponding with the person's name?"

"Got me."

Disappointed that the address book yielded no secrets, she threw it onto the coffee table. "Now what?"

"Now we sleep on it."

"Later, maybe," Marissa said, discouraged that he had offered no new ideas. "Right now, I have to check on Kamiko. And you can go do whatever it is you do when you're not working."

"If I didn't know better, I'd think you were trying to get rid of me."

If she thought Riley was going to continue arguing the point, he didn't. He merely gave her one of those odd, intense looks that sent chills up her spine before he quietly left. And Marissa knew that checking on Kamiko alone wouldn't do the trick for her. She was wide-awake. Maybe a swim with the dolphin would relax her.

LOOSE, WET, DARK HAIR streaming down her back, water rolling off her skin, the Gilmore woman appeared totally relaxed as she hopped up onto the boardwalk. Circling the isolation pen, the dolphin clicked and whistled at her. She adjusted her two-piece Lycra suit, positioned her toes over the boards and poised herself for another graceful dive.

Splash!

In she went, hell-bent on making it to the other side fast, oblivious of the danger looking over her shoulder. It would be perfect, really, her drowning right here, in one of the refuge enclosures with her beloved dolphin. Much better than in the bay.

Such a tragic accident...and while she was doing the work she was so dedicated to...

COMING UP FOR AIR, Marissa whirled around and tread water, her gaze trying to pierce the darkness cloaking the area beyond the boardwalk.

Nothing.

All night she'd been seeing absolutely nothing.

All night her imagination had been running wild.

So what was she supposed to do—find someplace to hide from fears both real and imagined? She'd be damned before she'd run.

A movement along her hip both startled her into swallowing a mouthful of water and reminded her that she was not alone.

"Kamiko, you're as bad as he is!"

He being the owner of Dolphin Haven, who seemed to enjoy startling her. For as much as she'd tried forgetting about him for a while, the task proved impossible.

As if her thinking about him had conjured him up, Riley stood poised above her, his sleek, near-nude body breathtaking in its magnificence. And then he sliced through the air, entered the water and came up alongside her.

"No wonder I felt eyes on me," she muttered, speculating on how long he'd been out there spying.

"You looked like you were having such fun, I had to join you."

"Fun?" she echoed. Cast in moonlight, his expression seemed pretty serious to her. "You mean *you* indulge in fun?"

"I have my moments."

So did she, and this was one of them. Moments of craziness. She wanted to forget about dead bodies and possible new dangers to her, wanted to celebrate life instead. And love.

For no matter how much she wanted to deny it, she was falling in love with Riley O'Hare.

They swam a few lengths together, Kamiko butting in between them and demanding attention. On opposite sides, both of them hung on to her dorsal fin and allowed her to drive them through the water at breakneck speed. Eventually the dolphin grew bored with the game and sought more challenging company—the two females and calf who watched from the other side of the fence. Marissa took the hint and opened the gate between the two pens. Kamiko immediately shot through.

"Hmm, she prefers dolphin to human company," Riley said as the small pod immediately lost all interest in them.

"So I've noticed." Marissa resecured the gate. "Away from the pressures of performing, she's doing fine."

"Which means your work here is done."

Did he want her to leave? She searched his face for a clue but couldn't tell. "Not quite." Could he possibly be so invulnerable that he could ignore their mutual attraction? "I can't go back yet." He was as much a reason as finding the murderer was.

"No, you can't." His deep-timbred tone sent ripples to her nerve endings.

Without Marissa having any clue of what he was up to, Riley placed his hands on her shoulders and, with a bounce in the water to give him drive, determinedly shoved her far under the surface. Too surprised to do more than hold her breath, Marissa sank without a fight. Eyes burning against the salty seawater, she nevertheless held them wide open as the silhouette that was Riley followed down on top of her. His hands were sliding around her neck . . . his thumbs resting on her windpipe . . .

Stunned, she froze, even as her pulse intensified against his fingers. Did he really mean to kill her?

Fear erupted into action. Her hands shot up to pry his away, her legs kicked frantically, banging against his, yet driving them both upward. As they broke the surface, his hands still firmly, if gently, around her neck, he dragged her head forward and sealed her lips with his.

The breath she was holding exploded into his mouth. His legs wrapped around her thighs. He was trying to seduce her, not kill her! Pulsating desire instantly replaced the momentary terror. She returned his kiss with all the longing and passion she'd stored away for far too long.

Suddenly Riley released her, only to push her against the underwater fence. Breathing heavily, he grasped the chain link on either side of her head.

"Having fun yet?" she said with a gasp, curling her fingers around the fencing at her hip for stability. Not that she could move if she wanted to. Which she didn't.

"Getting the hang of it," he agreed, dark hair plastered to his forehead.

When his head came toward hers, she let her eyes drift closed and savored this next kiss. He freed a hand to explore her through the Lycra suit. And beneath it. His fingers inched down below her waist along her cool flesh, igniting a fire deep inside her.

And when they found the center of her heat, he moaned into her mouth, "I want you."

Aware of the proof against her flesh, she murmured, "I know."

"Now."

"I know."

"Here."

"Then what are you waiting for?"

She helped him remove her bottom half as well as his own suit, his sensuous actions accentuated by his lips nuzzling her neck, then his teeth nipping her breasts until her hardened nipples thrust at her suit's top... and his exposed, hardened flesh prodded her thighs. With a deep breath, she parted her legs, offering him entrance, and again grasped the chain link for support as he slipped inside her.

For a while, they allowed the sea's gentle current to set their lazy rhythm. Marissa wrapped her legs around Riley's hips. His hands free, he explored every inch of her thoroughly. She watched him through half-closed eyelids. For once it seemed his expression was open. And deep in his eyes... she recognized a desire as strong as her own.

And unexpectedly urgent.

His expression changed subtly, its strength and mystery sending another chill through her. But there was nothing to fear, she told herself, banishing all images of snakes and freezer doors and motorcycles, banishing all memories of waterlogged bodies with gaping mouths and staring eyes....

For this one night, this one moment in time, this one watery adventure, she was safe in Riley's arms. To prove it, she pushed herself from the fence, wrapped her arms around his neck and kissed him hard. She could feel his legs treading to keep them afloat, his hands cupping her buttocks to lift her slightly as he speeded up his motion. They became one with nature. One with the current.

She hit high tide and finally knew what it felt like to experience *the little death*.

Chapter Eleven

"Death isn't a pleasant solution to anyone's problems," Riley coldly informed Cole Glaser after an early breakfast the next morning. "But it is effective. And permanent."

The swine had cornered him on his own property, near the toolshed on the far side of the pens, and Riley was worried that someone might stumble on them and figure things out. He couldn't help putting the fear of God into Glaser—it was taking all his willpower to keep his anger to mere words.

Hazel eyes narrowing—giving a pinched look to the youthful face that inspired too much trust in too many people—Glaser sneered, "Are you threatening me?"

"What do you think?"

"I think I want more money."

"And I think you've had more than enough."

"Are you ready to risk it all, O'Hare?" Glaser's boy-next-door appearance was only a facade. "Your precious refuge? Maybe your freedom?" The ruthless nature that made him so good at his job quickly came to the fore. His expression hardened to steel when he said, "Because if you are... hey, I'm a gambling man. Let's call that nice Detective Nick Lujan

over in Miami Beach and let him in on all our little secrets. What do you have to say to that?''

"I say you've been a lucky man...until now." Riley
wanted to wring the creep's neck with his bare hands,
to see the life force drain from his venal little mind.
"And that you shouldn't push your luck."

"You think about it." Glaser backed off. "I'll even
give you forty-eight hours. You have a sweet situation
here. Why ruin it? You can't do anything for your
precious dolphins from a jail cell, now can you?
Though someone really should pay for Dori's murder."

Riley lunged at him, but anticipating his reaction,
Glaser was already off, laughing to himself as he
jogged down the path toward the resort. Riley stared
after him, his gut churning, his breath coming fast and
harsh.

"Does Cole Glaser have some valid reason to think
you killed Dori?"

At the sound of Marissa's voice, Riley spun around
and gave her a black look vivid enough to replace
words—not that it satisfied her.

"Does he?" she asked again.

"Glaser's a pimple on the earth's—" Shaking his
head, Riley shouldered his way past her and went inside to get the toolbox he'd come for, as if ignoring the
question would make it go away. "Think what you
want to think. You will, anyway."

"How dare you!"

She was standing in the doorway, arms crossed
protectively in front of her breasts, cover-up reaching
nearly to her knees, hair confined in a prim braid, as
if she was hiding from her own sensuality.

"I think I dare pretty good," he said, thinking of the scene in the isolation pen the night before.

They had to be in sync because she said, "I thought we shared something special last night."

"We did." Bent on forcing her to back off, he carefully inspected the contents of the toolbox, and added, "Fun."

Her face drained of color. "Is that all it was to you?"

Her reaction got to him, made him want to take her in his arms and tell her— But he never should have gotten so close in the first place. He was no damn good at *close*. Among other things.

"Let me put it another way." The slight tremor in her voice was the only indication that her emotions were involved. Her posture and expression had both turned truculent. "If you *don't* tell me, I'll go to Detective Lujan and—"

"Keep out of this, Marissa!"

Riley wanted to slash out at something, but losing his temper never did make him feel any better. Still, he slammed down the lid of the toolbox and secured it.

"I won't."

He could tell she meant business. "All right." The sound of voices carried to him. Vida and Ken and Luke reporting for duty. He and his son were going to work on that gate for Brutus. "But not here."

"Where, then? And when?"

He thought quickly. "After lunch. We can take a walk around the island. Away from curious ears."

Riley only hoped he could trust Marissa. He'd gone that route with Dori. What a mistake. Now Dori would never be able to tell another soul.

MARISSA'S HEART WELLED with sadness as she set off with Riley later that day. After what they'd shared the night before, she'd been certain he had some feelings for her. But she'd been forced to reassess their relationship in light of Riley's attitude. She'd had to blackmail him into agreeing to talk. He was as distant and antagonistic as he'd been at first.

As they passed Toby Hanson's property, she was anxious to press for answers, but she held her questions for the moment. Hanson himself sat on his front porch. And when he spotted them, he rose from his rocker and deliberately stood at the porch rail to glare at them.

"Hanson doesn't like you much, does he?" Marissa observed.

"Hanson doesn't like anyone much. If he could, he'd buy out this whole island and live like some kind of damn primitive king."

Remembering how disagreeable Riley's neighbor had been to her, she could imagine the go-arounds between the two men. "But you don't even own the refuge land."

"No, not exactly." He clammed up and walked faster.

A few minutes later, they reached a tiny bay where a variety of birds, including herons and pelicans, fished for their lunches. Seaweed coated the shoreline, a broken, charcoal gray encrustation of dead coral. They sat on a felled mahogany tree trunk, and for a moment watched the antics of an egret. The peculiar bird on stilted legs eyed a minnow in the shallows, then chased it in a frenzy of lurching and splashing, flapping his wings and clacking his bill until he exhausted the tiny fish enough to seize it.

Marissa couldn't summon up enough energy to smile. "So what is going on, Riley?" she demanded to know without preamble. "Why is Cole Glaser blackmailing you?"

From the way he was staring out at the bay, his features as hard as she'd ever seen them, she didn't think he was going to answer. She couldn't summon up anger, either. Only a quickly growing disappointment.

And then he said, "He knows my real name—Riley O'Hare Strong." His granite face turned toward hers. "And that Ward Strong is my father."

"Ward Strong?" she echoed, thinking she should recognize the name.

"Owner of Marathon Fisheries."

She blinked. The newspaper...the articles she'd never managed to quite finish...but she'd read enough. "Oh my God, the company being sued by Ocean Watch."

"One and the same."

Then she made another connection. "Strong... Luke's last name. I should have put a couple of things together for myself." However, not understanding Riley's forsaking his legal name, she asked, "But why hide the fact? To get even with your father?" He'd made it clear they'd always been at odds.

He looked at her as if she wasn't thinking straight. "Here I am running a refuge for dolphins, while my father's fleet is still killing them in illegal numbers in tuna nets."

She frowned. "No one would blame *you* for his company's actions."

"No, but being linked with my father would go a long way toward destroying my credibility. I can't let that can't happen now, not when Dolphin Haven is up for a grant from Ocean Watch. If I don't get it . . ."

"There are other ways to support the refuge."

"We've been over this."

"But you haven't thought it through."

"I've done more thinking than you could imagine. I need the money fast or I'll lose the refuge altogether. As it stands, my lease is about up, and I'm several payments behind."

"Because of Cole Glaser?"

"Blackmail is expensive," he admitted. "If I don't keep paying Glaser's resort tabs—keep him on a permanent vacation, so to speak—the story will be all over the front page of that rag, *The National Citizen.* In case you haven't uncovered it yet, Glaser's a roving reporter with a nose for dirt."

No wonder Riley had been so hostile and potentially violent with the man. No wonder Glaser always seemed to be watching her. Going for another scoop? Another chunk of hush money?

"Can't you get the owner of the land to cut you some slack?" she asked.

Riley laughed ironically. "Just to complicate things further, the owner is the infamous Ward Strong himself."

"Your father owns the refuge?"

"Only the *land,*" he emphasized. "Mother talked him into a lease-buy option plan that holds as long as I meet my payments. He didn't think I'd even last the first year. I'm sure he envisioned me failing miserably and crawling back to him, begging for a job with Marathon Fisheries."

Knowing who his father was gave her a clearer picture of the parent-child animosity. If she and Riley clashed when they were really two versions of the same side, she could imagine what went on between him and his father.

"You wouldn't have to work for your father no matter what," she insisted, not knowing why she was trying to make him feel better when he obviously hadn't wanted to share any of this with her in the first place. "You're highly respected and could get a job working with..." Realizing what she was about to suggest, she faltered.

"One of the big parks with performing dolphins?" he finished for her. "You see how the idea kind of goes against the grain, I hope."

Dropping that line of thought, she went back to the blackmail. "So how did Glaser find out?"

Riley was silent so long it spooked her. Finally he said, "I made the mistake of telling Dori. Is this another mistake—telling you?"

That hauntingly familiar crawly sensation slid along her spine. Marissa tried not to interpret his tone as threatening. She tried not to think of all those times someone had tried to kill her, times when only Riley happened to be nearby.

He was here now...and they were alone...and she wondered why he'd chosen this deserted place to tell her the truth.

"That depends on what you mean by mistake," she said hoarsely.

His gaze bore into her, making her nervous. "Who do you plan on telling?"

Heart beating in her throat, she said, "No one."

"Good. That's good."

Imagining his tone was more sinister than mellifluous, Marissa was hard-pressed not to react by rubbing the gooseflesh spreading along her arms. She stared at Riley and saw not the man she'd made love with the night before, but a stranger.

"So that was Dori's big secret about the land...your father's owning it."

"I didn't murder her."

"I didn't say you did."

"You were thinking it, though." Before she could respond, he added, "Losing the refuge might kill *me*, but I'd never kill anyone else over it."

Some of her tension dissipated with Riley's denial. Marissa wanted to believe him—*did* believe him!—and only hoped she wasn't fooling herself.

"Then who would?" Only one name came to mind. "If Dori was upset enough by your breaking up with her to share the information with other people," she said, "then your secret would be public knowledge and Cole Glaser would lose an easy source of income."

As far as she was concerned, a man capable of blackmail might also be capable of murder.

"I'M CAPABLE OF DOING the work. You know that!" Vida argued with Riley late that afternoon. "What do you think I've been doing for the past week?"

Marissa couldn't help overhearing the altercation. No one in the area could. The blonde had horned in on the time Riley was spending with his son. He and Luke were just finishing installing the gate to the bay from the main pen, and Vida stood over him on the boardwalk.

"We'll discuss this later," Riley said calmly, boosting himself up out of the water.

"No. *Now*. I just heard Amanda Hopkins was coming down first thing next week."

"That's right. I invited her."

"So you could give her the marine mammal specialist's job that's rightfully mine?"

"Rightfully?" he echoed, his tone incredulous.

"You told me I should be patient and keep learning while I did all the grunt work around here. Well, I've done that, haven't I? And don't I do a good job of filling in whenever I'm needed?" When Riley refused to respond, Vida shouted, "Dori is dead! Get over it! Now it's my turn!"

Even the irrepressibly cheerful Ken was shocked. He made a strangled sound, and his freckles turned nearly as red as his hair against his pale face. "Uh-oh, she's done it now," he whispered to Marissa.

"We'll discuss this later," Riley said again, only this time his features were dark with barely controlled anger. *"In private!"*

Marissa was surprised that he kept his temper so well.

With a squeal, Vida spun on her heel and stalked off, her expression one of blind rage. So blind, she knocked into Marissa. Helpless against the tall woman's weight, Marissa teetered on the edge of the boardwalk and practically fell into the pen. She caught herself just in time.

"You'll be sorry, Riley O'Hare!" Vida was shouting over her shoulder. "You've underestimated me once too often."

A threat? And her earlier words finally struck home. *Get over it?* What a heartless thing to say about someone's death. Every so often, Vida revealed a side of herself that really put Marissa off. She was getting the strong feeling that Vida Dalberg would do almost anything to get what she wanted—exactly what she'd accused Dori of.

Suddenly an image flew into her mind. Vida and Cole Glaser together at Lime Tree Resort. She hadn't remembered until this very moment. Though she wasn't certain what to make of it, she felt Riley should know. She'd be sure to inform him first chance she got.

Which wouldn't be soon, since he said something to Luke in a low tone and stalked off in the opposite direction.

Rubbing at the arm Vida had smacked into, Marissa stiffened. At six feet, Vida was definitely large enough to knock her on her fanny, whether here or on a beach. And in the dark, and wearing a wet suit and related gear, definitely large enough to be mistaken for a man.

Could it be? Could Vida have wanted Dori's job badly enough to kill her?

Before remembering about the scuba diver, she hadn't assumed anything about the killer's sex. Hadn't she told Riley it could be a woman? Maybe it had been. Maybe Vida had gotten rid of her competition. But killing someone to advance a career? Was it really likely?

As likely as Cole Glaser killing Dori to keep Riley's background an exclusive for blackmail.

Billie's arrival at the pens distracted her. She'd seen the housekeeper in the area only once...with Erasmus North.

"Marissa, that Detective Lujan's here," the housekeeper said. "He wants to see you and Riley."

"He can see me. You'll have to scare up your employer. He stalked off a few minutes ago. He went thataway," she said, indicating the direction of the toolshed.

Throwing on her big T-shirt, Marissa rushed back to the house, vaguely aware that Billie shambled along behind her instead of looking for Riley. Dressed in orange shorts and an orange shirt with purple flowers, Detective Nick Lujan was sprawled on the deck, sucking on a mug of coffee.

Coming up for air, he saluted her. "Miss Gilmore."

"Have you rounded up anything new, Detective?" Marissa asked before he could state his purpose. "I assume you've been too busy with this case to contact me as you promised you would—you're two days late."

Rather than excusing himself, he said, "I've been doing background checks on all the people you mentioned the other night."

"And?"

"Squat. They're all clean."

Though she wasn't surprised the culprit didn't have a record, she said, "One of them certainly isn't clean. One of them tried to kill me again, this time with a motorcycle on Key West."

He sat up straighter. "I didn't hear about another attempt. And you reported this, right?"

She glanced toward the house. Was that shadow on the other side of the screen door Billie? "Only Riley knows." Or so she thought.

"That makes lotsa sense."

Irritated by his sarcasm, she returned, "As much sense as it did reporting the first three attempts to you."

"You didn't follow my advice and go home, now, did you?"

"Who's to say I would have been safer anywhere else?"

He took another slug of coffee and stared at her as if he were trying to get inside her head. "So, have you remembered yet?" he asked in a low voice, his gaze flashing to the screen door, warning her that someone was, indeed, listening.

"What?"

Continuing in a tone too low to be heard more than a few feet away, he said, "Whatever it is that's making the murderer come after you."

She hesitated only a second. "Maybe."

"Shoot."

"The night Dori was killed," she said softly, glancing back at the house, "I was pacing up and down the beach calling for Kamiko." No one was there now...at least no one that she could see.

"I've heard this part before," Lujan stated.

"What you haven't heard is the part about the scuba diver."

"What scuba diver?"

"The one who came out of the surf and crashed into me. We fell down onto the sand together. Something of the diver's was caught on my wet suit. Finding that something made me remember the incident."

"I'm spellbound," he said, setting down his mug. "What was it you found?"

"A tiny metal shark. The Predator insignia."

He cursed. "Now all we have to do is find a diver who uses Predator equipment. Yeah, that narrows it down to a few thousand in this area."

"There aren't a few thousand people on this key."

He nodded as if giving her a point. "Look, why didn't you tell me about this as soon as you remembered?"

Wanting to avoid telling Lujan that she'd known when she and Riley had met with him in Miami Beach, Marissa hedged. "Why didn't you call?"

"Touché." Lujan sat forward. "You wouldn't have seen anyone around here wearing Predator equipment?"

She shook her head. "I haven't been diving with anyone else. I did find a Predator buoyancy compensator on the refuge boat, but the shark was intact."

"It belonged to O'Hare?"

"No. Too small."

He flashed her what she guessed must be his tough-guy expression. "You know, Miss Gilmore, I gotta read you the hard-liner on this. Leave the investigation to the pros."

"Can you guarantee you'll find the murderer before he gets another chance at me?"

"I was only quoting official policy. If you know anything else, you'd be smart to share it with me."

She thought about telling him of their visit to Mrs. Lynch and about the woman's claim that Dori's secret had something to do with the land. But that would lead to other revelations. That would mean she'd have to betray Riley. And she'd sworn she wouldn't.

"No, nothing else, Detective Lujan." She only hoped she wouldn't have cause to regret her loyalty. "Sorry."

It was only after he left that she remembered finding the note that led to the cabin where she'd found what she'd assumed was Dori's address book. Not that it had been of any help. Still, first thing on returning to her quarters, she dug out the small leather-bound notebook, made herself comfortable on the couch and gave it a more thorough once-over.

The result was the same as last time. Too few entries and not enough knowledge to make anything of them.

Marissa thumbed to the back page where the two series of numbers had been penciled in. On impulse, she decided to call the first. She punched in the seven digits, waited through three rings, and then listened to a woman's cheerful voice answer with, "Key Developers."

Developers?

A catch in her throat, Marissa said, "I'm not certain I've reached the right company. What is it exactly that you do?"

"We oversee land development projects from Key Largo to Key West," the woman chirped.

Land! "As in a real estate office?"

"More like a design-construction business."

Confused, Marissa dropped the receiver into its cradle. Why would Dori Lynch have scribbled down the number of land developers? And why enter it in her address book without identifying the company?

Riley should know about this.

Before leaving to find him, however, she tried dialing the other number, using the same prefix with the four digits Riley had suggested might be an extension or fax number. But the only answer she received was a recorded message from the phone company, informing her that the number was not in service.

Maybe the digits were part of an address. Eight-five-four-seven ... Though something was familiar about the combination, she couldn't put her finger on it.

Marissa thought she'd better find a clever hiding place for the address book. A rap at the door made her jump, and she barely managed to shove the thin volume between the couch cushions before the door swung open to reveal Riley, wearing a ferocious expression and startling her nearly out of her mind.

"You leave your door unlocked after someone tries to kill you countless times?"

"You just walk into someone's living quarters without so much as a by-your-leave?" she demanded in return. Then she tried lightening up her own temper. "Four. *I've* been keeping count." And she wondered how, indeed, she could have forgotten to deadbolt her door. Not only her nerves, but also her concentration seemed to be fraying.

"Cute." He slammed the door closed and stood there, still seeming ticked off. And suspicious. "So Lujan was here. What did you tell him?"

Though she didn't like the implication in his words or tone, she forced herself to keep calm. "About the scuba diver and shark."

"That's it?"

"Pretty much." Before he could say something she might take offense at, Marissa offered, "I didn't say a word about the land or about your father if that's what you're worried about."

"One of the things."

She didn't ask him about the others. "Sit. I have some information."

He moved closer, though he didn't take her up on her invitation. "Lujan did some detecting?"

"*I* did some detecting."

"How? When? I saw you barely an hour ago."

"But that's before I placed a very important phone call. To Key Developers."

He grimaced. "I don't understand."

"I called the number in Dori's book—the one penciled in on the back page."

"Key Developers," he repeated slowly, as if letting the connection sink in.

"They develop land in the Florida Keys. A design and construction company. Dori's secret?"

Riley practically fell onto the couch. "She must really have hated me if she was trying to sell me out."

"You don't think she was personally involved with this company?"

"Why not?"

"I...don't know. It hadn't occurred to me."

She supposed it should have, considering the things that Billie and Vida and Riley had been saying about her all along.

"Then who?" Riley asked.

"What about Toby Hanson? What if he objects to the refuge not because it's a bother, but because he wants to make some kind of deal with these developers?"

"Dori didn't even know Hanson other than as someone to be avoided," Riley insisted. "And supposing it was Hanson, then how did those numbers get in *her* address book?"

That did put a kink in things. But she couldn't help fishing. "Someone got her pregnant. Are you absolutely sure it couldn't have been Toby Hanson?"

"She wouldn't have gone with that ape after..."

"What? You?"

"I don't see it. I just don't." He shook his head and struck the back of the couch with a fist. Marissa stood up and began to pace the floor. "None of this makes any damn sense!"

It didn't, Marissa agreed. More and more. "No more sense than your believing Dori betrayed you," she said slowly, turning toward him as an idea occurred to her.

"She did betray me—to Cole Glaser!"

"Are you certain?" She thought about Dori's bungalow. "Dori seemed to be a real romantic—"

"A few feminine things didn't make her a perfect person."

"I didn't say perfect. Romantic. Idealistic. It seems to me she was both."

He seemed uneasy. "So?"

"That description doesn't fit with a woman who could turn around and not only brutally betray you, but her charges, as well. If Key Developers is able to get hold of refuge land, what will happen to the dolphins?"

Riley made a sound of deep frustration. "I guess she didn't give a damn!"

"Didn't she?" The few times she'd met Dori, Marissa had been convinced of the other woman's absolute dedication to her work. "Are you certain Glaser didn't find out about you some other way?"

"Dori was the only one who knew!"

"Not Billie?"

"Yes, Billie, of course, but I'd trust her with my life," he stated, rising from the couch and stepping so close she could see the knotted cords of his neck.

Refusing to be intimidated, Marissa went on, "Did Dori ever admit she was guilty?"

That question brought the conversation to a dead halt. Riley stared at her and finally said, "No. Actually, she denied it."

"But you couldn't trust her." Because he couldn't trust any woman since his ex-wife had betrayed him, marrying him for money that he might never have, leaving him when she realized he wasn't going for the gold ring?

"I saw her talking to Glaser just before he put the squeeze on me," Riley said.

"And *I* saw Vida talking to Glaser."

He merely stared.

"I saw them together at the restaurant. They were acting very cozy."

His voice was deceptively soft and cool when he asked, "What made you suddenly decide to tell me this?"

"I wasn't keeping it from you purposely." She could sense his rising anger.

"Not like the scuba diver and shark, right?"

Refusing to let him put her on the defensive, Marissa asked, "Are you bound and determined to start a fight, or what?"

"I could ask the same of you!"

"And I could ask you to leave!"

"You won't have to ask twice." With that, he stormed toward the door.

"Riley, don't be ridiculous!" She wanted to eat the word as soon as it came out of her mouth—"ridiculous" was right up there with "fool" and "idiot." "Please, don't leave."

But he already had one foot out the door. "Lock up tight. Your next visitor might not be so amiable!"

Waiting until he slammed the door behind him, she yelled, "Control freak!" He couldn't stand not having things his way—not even an argument.

And at the moment, she couldn't stand him. Better that he did leave now, while she still had enough sense left to know that they had absolutely no future together, anyhow.

"WORKING LATE?"

The irritating voice of Cole Glaser stopped her halfway down the path toward the refuge. Having skipped dinner altogether, Marissa had napped for several hours and was now on her way back to the dolphin pens.

"What's it to you?"

"Friendly question."

"Right. You're full of friendly questions." She wondered if he'd been waiting for her to leave her cabin or if running into him was a coincidence. For some reason, she didn't think much of what Glaser did could be chalked up to happenstance. "How many answers make it to *The National Citizen?*"

"Only the really interesting ones."

Marissa wondered why her pulse didn't do more than speed up a bit. It was dark, and here she was in the middle of this semitropical jungle alone with Glaser. She was on the alert but not hyperventilating. He was definitely a blackmailer. For all she knew, he could be the killer. Maybe it was because she'd seen him at Riley's mercy that she couldn't exactly muster up a healthy amount of fear.

"Turnabout is fair play, isn't it?" she asked boldly. "So I have a question for you."

He shrugged. "Shoot." He appeared kind of amused.

"Why did you let Riley think Dori spilled the beans about his father?"

Glaser was clearly taken aback. His eyes went round and his mouth gaped for a second...but he made a quick save. "She *did*."

Taking her best guess, Marissa suggested, "But not to you, right? Funny, but I never got the impression that Dori and Vida were close enough friends to share secrets."

A flickering behind his eyes told her she'd hit a nerve. *Bingo—Vida*. That was it. The jealous co-worker befriending Dori only to wangle Riley's secret from her. Maybe she'd been looking for leverage to get the job she wanted, but the information had proved even more valuable. Marissa could well imagine it. She could also bluff with the best of them.

"You'd better tell your girlfriend to be careful," she said. "Riley might appreciate the truth, but he'll think even less of Vida when I tell him how she let poor Dori take the blame for something she didn't do."

Without waiting for his reaction, she spun around and stalked off toward the refuge. Only when she got inside the perimeter fence did she allow herself to turn back. Glaser was nowhere to be seen. She let out the breath she hadn't realized she'd been holding.

Maybe she was a little afraid, at that.

Gathering a bucket of fish she'd set in a refrigerator earlier—no way would she go into the freezer herself—she made for the pens where she separated

Kamiko from the other dolphins using the underwater gate.

"Feel like doing a few tricks?" she asked, displaying her whistle, the sound of which created a bridge between the dolphin's correct response to a trainer's signal and the food reward to follow. Basically it was meant to tell the dolphin "great job!"

Kamiko turned sideways to eye her and made a series of clicking noises. Marissa wasn't certain whether or not that was approval, but she was pretty sure Kamiko understood. Since arriving, she'd kept her time with the dolphin mostly for play, but now she wanted to see her reaction to a request for some serious work.

Work they could both use—Kamiko to stay in fighting form, Marissa to get her mind off Riley.

First she used an open hand as a simple target. The dolphin tapped Marissa's palm with her nose. Marissa gave a sharp blow on the whistle and tossed her a fish. Immediately attentive, Kamiko waited for the next signal. Marissa turned her hand over, and the dolphin rolled over and flopped her flipper against the water's surface. Another whistle and fish.

When Kamiko became distracted, ignoring her next signal, Marissa thought perhaps someone had come to watch. She looked around, but they were alone, unless someone was hiding in the shadow of a palm tree. Attention split between her surroundings and the dolphin, Marissa tried again. This time, no problem. She relaxed.

Within minutes, Kamiko was doing a series of jumps and bows and seemed to enjoy the tricks as much as the rewards. If only that could last, she thought, hoping the dolphin could learn to enjoy performing for big crowds on a daily basis once she was shipped back to the oceanarium.

She made a big V with both hands, and the dolphin did a one-and-a-half-turn somersault.

As the whistle and the splashing sounds died away, Marissa thought she heard another noise nearby. A familiar-sounding *clunk*. She froze and listened hard, then was chastised by Kamiko, who demanded her reward. Marissa gave her the remaining fish and signaled the end of the workout.

She waited for another noise. When none came but the clicking of the other dolphins who were unusually talkative, she shook away the weird feeling and slipped into the pen. A soft *thunk* against the wall of the pen next to them indicated one of the animals was a little uptight.

Kamiko brushed her side. Marissa began swimming, the dolphin alongside her for a few minutes. But it soon became clear that something was agitating Kamiko. She whistled and clicked and suddenly did a one-eighty that nearly knocked Marissa under.

"What in the heck's going on?" she said breathlessly, the only words out of her mouth before something—someone—grasped her ankles and pulled.

Chapter Twelve

Marissa closed her eyes, held her breath, and allowed herself to be pulled underwater thinking that Riley had somehow sneaked into the pen and was playing another seduction game with her. Only when the hold around her ankles didn't loosen, when she felt herself being dragged toward the bottom of the pen while her lungs began to protest, did she become seriously alarmed.

She opened her eyes against the water, squinting against the salt burn, barely able to make out a dark, bulky figure below her. Heart pounding, she squeezed her lids shut and gave her lower body a huge twist that managed to free one of her legs. She kicked and clawed her way to the surface, despite the pressure on her other still-captive ankle. Somehow, the water being an equalizer between individuals of varying strengths, she made it.

But one fast gasp for air and she was dragged under once more. She quickly realized that her attacker was no mere swimmer who would also need air. The person was staying below the surface and, therefore, must be breathing from a tank.

The scuba diver!

What chance did she have against someone so well equipped? A diver could sit at the bottom until the tank ran out, a half hour or more. And she would be long dead before that, unless she figured out something fast.

Her pulse rate soared as she willfully kept her free leg out of the diver's reach and used her hands to fan herself upward. Carefully she inserted the whistle between her teeth even as she broke the surface. She sucked in some air and let out a series of powerful whistle blasts meant to alert any nearby humans that she needed help. All the while, she struggled to free her other leg to no avail.

The hand fastened around it twisted abruptly and wrenched her whole body. The whistle flew out of her mouth, but luckily she was able to swallow more air before being pulled under a third time.

Third time's the charm...

She couldn't believe that, not even when she swallowed a mouthful of salt water. Not if she wanted to live. The bastard had tried to kill her more times than that and she wasn't through fighting yet.

Suddenly a smooth body cut through the water along her side, renewing her hope. *Kamiko!* The dolphin reminded Marissa she wasn't alone.

On impulse, she used her arms to help shove her weight downward *toward* the diver, her free foot flailing for the head. Her strategy worked. The grip on her ankle loosened and a hand tried powerlessly to clutch her other leg. She continued kicking, her lungs beginning to burn as her heel finally came into contact with the diver's mask, successfully dislodging it and giving the diver something to worry about—her breaking the seal meant it was filling with water. Too bad she hadn't gotten the regulator so the villain couldn't breathe.

But the mask proved to be good enough.

Suddenly she was free... and zooming in out of nowhere, Kamiko hooked her bottlenose under Marissa's arm to push her to the surface. Coughing up seawater as her face hit the night air, feeling as if her lungs had been close to bursting, she rasped out, "Good girl!"

Leaving her be, the dolphin sped across the pen while Marissa tried to catch her breath and regain her strength, knowing the confrontation wasn't over yet.

Seconds later, the diver was on the attack, this time coming to the surface. Though Marissa tried, she couldn't recognize the face behind the mask in such poor light. And no sooner did a gloved hand reach for her, than a silver gray bullet struck the diver in the side. Kamiko again. The black-garbed body went sailing along the water toward the other pens... then jerked and spun in the other direction.

Marissa cleared her eyes and quickly looked around. The water surrounding her was unexpectedly churning with sleek, silver gray bodies! Responding to the danger and possibly her trainer's whistle—her signature whistle giving out a sound of distress—they'd come to her rescue.

With frenzied clicking, the dolphins played keep away; only this time, the diver was the object they were keeping away from her.

The frantic activity drew farther away toward the other pens, making Marissa believe she'd escaped with her life once more. Panting, sucking in the night air for all she was worth, she wondered what the killer would do next. Then activity suddenly ceased, and the dolphins calmly circled the pen, their more regulated noises making them sound quite satisfied with themselves.

Marissa looked for a body, but of course there was none. The dolphins weren't killers as the scuba diver was. She realized her attacker had escaped by back-tracking through the series of underwater gates, exiting through the new one Riley and Luke had just installed between the bay and the main pen. Obviously the gates had been opened to serve as the diver's escape hatch, but they'd also given easy access to the pens' occupants.

"Thank God," she muttered, her energy draining away.

She felt weak. Boneless. Couldn't move except to listlessly tread water. Didn't do anything more for several minutes.

A nudge sent her toward land. Then two dolphins offered her escort—Kamiko and Brutus. Gratefully she clung to their dorsal fins and allowed them to swim her to the boardwalk, where they both rose slightly out of the water to give her the boost she wasn't certain she could manage by herself. She found a handhold and dragged herself up onto the planks, where she collapsed on her side.

In the water, Kamiko tilted her head to stare out of one eye. Marissa dangled one hand over the side to pat both her charge and the other dolphins who swam by ostensibly to check on her.

"You're all getting extra fish from me personally," she promised when she'd recovered enough to talk. "Even if I have to go into that damned freezer to get them myself."

"What's this about the freezer?"

Nearly jumping out of her skin, she rolled onto her back and gaped up at Riley O'Hare. He was dressed in civilian clothes—shorts and a T-shirt—but his hair was wet. Her heart thundered in her breast.

Had the dolphins saved her from death in the sea only to deliver her to the murderer on land?

WHY THE HELL WAS MARISSA staring at him as if he was some kind of murderer? Riley frowned at her. She looked like a half-drowned rat—well, an attractive one who filled out an electric blue swimsuit very nicely.

"What's going on?" he asked, stooping next to her. Using a gentle finger, he swept back a dark strand of wet hair plastered to her cheek. She flinched. "What are all these dolphins doing in the isolation pen?" And why were her eyes all wide and weird on him?

"The murderer just tried to drown me," she told him, her voice rough, her body stiff. "He got into the pens using the underwater gates. The dolphins came to my rescue."

"What?" he boomed. "That's why you laid on the whistle?"

"You heard and didn't come?"

"I was in the shower. I got here as quickly as I could. Are you all right?"

Her expression gradually changed. Relaxed. "I am now."

What was that supposed to mean? He had the feeling she was talking about more than escaping with her life again. "You didn't think that *I* was trying to drown you?"

"Well, no."

But she sounded odd and wasn't looking straight at him. Her gaze was pinned at shoulder level. Disgusted that she still didn't trust him, he stood without offering her a hand.

"I'll take care of the dolphins."

"Riley..."

First he fetched flippers, snorkel, mask and underwater headlight. By the time he drew off his T-shirt
and donned the equipment, she was sitting upright.
Not looking very good, either.

"Here." He threw her the T-shirt. "Put it on.
You're turning blue at the gills."

Without waiting to see if she would do as he ordered, he jumped into the pen and, once in the water,
was immediately brushed by a solid body.

"No games tonight," he said gruffly, giving Brutus
a hand signal to dive and go through the gate.

The male did as ordered, two members of his harem
following. He slapped water until he got Pegeen's attention—she was the stubborn one—and had to give
her the same signal twice. With a saucy flip of her
fluke, she, too, went. That left the pregnant dolphin,
who followed on her own. The calf and mother had
never left their enclosure. Likewise the juveniles, since
the scuba diver hadn't had to come through their pen.

Since Kamiko was supposed to be on a rest cure, he
checked to make certain the incident hadn't rattled her
too badly. He called her over and stroked her, even
scratched her tongue when she opened her mouth for
the treat. Because he sensed her eyes boring into him,
he glanced at Marissa, who looked absolutely stricken.
And quickly glanced away.

Riley dived down through the underwater gate,
drawing it securely closed. The headlight lit the area,
and he made a thorough check of the sandy bottom
before continuing.

Then he sent Brutus and his three ladies through a
second gate to the main pen. None of the dolphins
seemed the least bit interested in the open gate to the
bay. Knowing the perversity of animals, Riley figured
that because he and Luke had installed an easy way

back in, Brutus would probably never choose to take an unauthorized stroll again.

He checked the remaining two through areas but came up empty-handed.

"Your scuba diver didn't leave anything behind this time," he said as he hauled himself up on the board-walk several yards from Marissa. She was wearing his T-shirt.

"Not my diver."

"Any idea who it might have been?" he asked, stripping off gear as he approached her. "Other than me, of course."

She shook her head. "Not enough light."

When it seemed as if she might be cemented to the damned boardwalk, he offered a hand. Giving him a frightened look, she took it and allowed him to help her up. He tried steeling himself against her, but it was no good. His arms acting of their own volition, they wrapped around her.

"I'm sorry," she whispered. "It just seemed like every time something...bad...happened to me, there you were. But I never really believed you were the one. Well, almost never."

Gently he covered her mouth with his hand. "Stop babbling before you get yourself into more trouble."

She covered his hand with her own, her lips brushing his palm. The light gesture of affection stirred him. He held her tighter. How many more attempts on her life could she survive? He didn't want to know. He didn't know how to protect her.

Her mouth pressed into his shoulder, and she suddenly said, "Dori didn't do it."

"Do what?"

"Betray you to Cole Glaser."

"Of course she did." She *had* to have. "There was no one else."

"It was Vida. She befriended Dori and got your secret out of her somehow. She's the one who told Glaser."

"He admitted that?"

"Not in so many words, but yes."

"When did you have this conversation?"

"On my way—"

"Here?" he finished for her. "Then he could have warned Vida."

"And if she was the murderer, she could have come after me."

"Let's find out."

He didn't want to take her, but he didn't know what else to do. He couldn't leave her alone. Not again. Maybe never again. Fool that he was, he'd gone and done it this time. Fallen in love.

When they got to Vida's bungalow, it was dark. Riley banged on the door. No answer. He tried the knob. It turned in his hand.

"Wait here," he cautioned Marissa, reaching in for the light switch.

But his caution was for naught. The bungalow was empty. Not only of Vida, but of her possessions, as well, as he learned after a quick search. She'd fled. Because she was guilty?

He stared into an empty closet. "She must be the one."

"I don't think so."

He turned to see Marissa standing in the doorway. "You're the one who suggested—"

"I could be wrong." She entered the bungalow and her eyes gave it a cursory sweep. "She didn't have enough time to try to drown me, then pack her things and steal away without anyone noticing."

"What if she was already packed?"

"You think she planned to kill me and disappear so the deed would point to her?"

"You're right," Riley conceded. "How the hell did she get off the island? The boat's been docked all day. And the skiff is gone."

Marissa shuddered. "Don't remind me. Vida probably picked up a ride back to Key Largo with a worker or visitor from the resort."

That, too, made sense. "So if she *isn't* the murderer, why did she leave at all?" Riley wondered aloud.

"You may have something to do with that." When Riley merely stared, Marissa said, "You wouldn't give her Dori's job. She'd gone through a lot of trouble— if not murder—to get it. She said you'd be sorry. Maybe she decided skipping out on you and leaving you shorthanded would serve you right."

"Maybe." If only he could be sure she wasn't up to more mischief.

"Why did you refuse to consider Vida for the job?"

"Instinct." And he'd been proven right. "Let's get out of here."

Marissa not only looked bedraggled but also exhausted. And vulnerable. Riley refused to allow her to put herself in further danger. Unbelievably, she didn't protest when he headed her straight for the main house rather than the resort. Nor did she resist when he insisted she stay the night.

They showered together, but a long, loving kiss was as far as he allowed his desire to take him. He helped Marissa pull on one of his T-shirts and, after getting into bed, tucked her snugly into his side.

Where he would keep her forever, if he could.

"Riley," she said, already sounding sleepy. "About my not trusting you—"

"It's all right."

"No, it's not. It's just that I was so scared my judgment was off. I'm truly sorry."

He hugged her closer, wanting nothing more than to make love to her. And she needed nothing less, so he didn't. Instead, he gave her comfort and security and the opportunity to sleep undisturbed.

He on the other hand, stayed awake half the night, puzzling the situation over in his mind. Though Vida had been involved, she wasn't a murderer, but the land was obviously the key. And to his knowledge, only one person had shown interest in buying.

Their next step would be to discover whether Toby Hanson had a working relationship with Key Developers.

"DON'T WORRY, IF Toby Hanson has something going with Key Developers, I'll find out somehow," Marissa said with only slightly more confidence than she was feeling.

Having finished their morning rounds with the dolphins as quickly as possible, they'd left Ken in charge and had made for Key Largo. Halfway across the bay, she'd spotted Erasmus North's old fishing boat sitting out in open water within what she guessed was binocular-spying distance of the refuge.

At the time, Riley hadn't taken the fact seriously. He was after Hanson with a vengeance. He now stared straight ahead, silently, as they drove through the streets of Key Largo.

Recognizing his control freak expression when she saw it, she insisted, "You *can't* go in," for at least the third time. "If they do recognize you, it's all over."

"I know, but I don't have to like it," he groused.

She muttered, "You can't keep me in sight every moment of every day."

"Why not?"

Their gazes locked and she didn't so much as blink as he pulled her into his arms for an aggressive kiss. She responded in kind, elated at the emotion she'd heard in his voice, at the possessive way he held her. It was beginning to feel as if she wasn't the only one madly in love here. For she *was* in love with Riley O'Hare, even if she didn't know where that would get her.

She broke the kiss and breathlessly said, "The sooner I get in there, the sooner we have an answer."

They were sitting in Riley's car outside a restaurant across the street from the development company's offices. Her adrenaline was surging. She felt a little dizzy at the prospect of finally putting a stop to the attempts on her life. At least now she knew for certain that Riley wasn't the one. If he had been, Kamiko never would have let him get close to her the night before—the dolphin would have become agitated instead.

Marissa wondered how she ever could have doubted Riley.

"All right, go then, but if there's any sign of trouble, scream."

She reached into the front of her dress and dragged out her dolphin whistle, which she was wearing on a thin gold chain. "This proved to be pretty effective last night."

He nodded. "Promise you won't take any chances."

"No chances," she agreed, sliding out of the car.

A blast of heat whomped her immediately upon hitting the pavement. The afternoon sun was blazing, the air humid and still. She was covered in sweat by the time she crossed the street and prepared to enter Key Developers. Plain on the outside—stucco painted a deep turquoise—the office itself was plush by comparison. Obviously some money had gone into the decor, a combination of island and Art Deco.

Her eyes wandered from the tropical prints in the sitting area to the broad shoulders of a fair-haired man disappearing into one of the inside offices. Something about the burly young man was familiar.

"May I help you?" a petite redhead at the front desk asked, interrupting her musing.

Marissa took in the chic salon haircut and the short-sleeved linen summer suit and realized Key Developers demanded a good-looking front, both in decor and personnel. Good thing she'd worn the one expensive dress and matching jacket she'd brought with her to Lime Key. In addition, she'd done up her hair in sophisticated French braids and had worn her only pair of real gold earrings.

Putting on a perky smile, Marissa held out her hand for a shake and said, "I'm Nicole Lujan." For some reason, the female version of the cop's name was the first thing that popped into her head. "I understand your firm develops properties all over the Keys."

"Yes, we do. You have a piece of land—"

"Looking for one."

The redhead pursed her mouth. "Sorry, but we're not a real estate agency. There is one right down the street, however."

"Been there, done that," Marissa said fliply. She took a seat to the side of the receptionist's desk and checked the engraved nameplate. Serita Cavanaugh. "The problem, Serita, is that no one seems to be able to help me."

"Well, I don't see how we can, either, considering we merely develop properties our clients bring to us."

Marissa gave the woman her most frustrated expression. "I was afraid you were going to say that. Maybe you know someone who could help me then."

Serita merely shrugged and seemed to want to get back to her paperwork.

"I mean, maybe you know someone who has land they're developing where I want to buy," Marissa pressed. "With the proper introduction, perhaps I can convince this person to sell me a teensy-weensy piece of property. Just enough for a little retreat."

Sighing in resignation, Serita asked, "Where exactly did you have in mind?"

"Lime Key."

The redhead's expression immediately tightened. "Sorry, we haven't done any business there. Lime Key is a closed commodity."

"Are you certain?" Marissa asked. She'd hit on something, she was certain of it. "I stayed at the resort this winter and really fell in love with the place."

"Even so, I doubt you would have the resources, uh, even if any land was available."

Her smile virtually triumphant, Marissa said, "My boyfriend is the one with the resources."

A door opening behind her drew Serita's full attention.

"I need those files on— Excuse me, I didn't know we had a client."

"Mr. D'Angelo, Nicole Lujan. She's looking to buy a piece of property on Lime Key, but I told her we're not a real estate office."

Marissa could hardly miss the tension in the other woman's voice. Curiosity made her turn. And freeze. Thin and dark and weathered, Mr. D'Angelo not only looked familiar, she could also place him exactly.

A FEW MINUTES LATER, Marissa left the office with barely a glance back. Serita Cavanaugh was watching her while making a telephone call. About her? Had D'Angelo recognized her, then?

Practically tripping in her rush to get across the street—she was more used to going barefoot than wearing three-inch heels—Marissa was panting by the time she threw herself into the car. "Let's get out of here!"

"What?" Riley demanded, starting the engine. "I didn't hear any damn whistle." He tore out of their parking spot. "By the way, where are we going?"

"Back to the harbor parking lot."

"You want to return to Lime Key right now?"

"Not until we check out something."

"Are you going to tell me what happened in there, or am I going to have to wring your neck to get it out of you? Is Hanson the one or not?"

She grinned at him. "I recognized the proprietor, Mr. D'Angelo. He and his buddy—more likely his bodyguard—were having an intense conversation with Ansel Roche the other night."

"What's Roche got to do with this?"

"Exactly." As they turned into the lot, she asked, "You know his car?"

"I know it."

"Find it."

"Then what?"

"Then we see what it can tell us. You did know that Ansel was consoling Dori after you broke up with her, didn't you?"

His silence told her that he had not. He didn't speak until he pulled up alongside the white Le Baron. "How do you plan on getting in? Do you possess criminal skills you haven't told me about?"

"Merely a good, if sometimes erratic, memory. Remember the four-digit number in Dori's address book?"

"No."

"I do. Eight-five-four-seven. The same keypad combination Ansel used to get into his car the night we went for a drink. I thought it seemed familiar...."

From the way he was glaring at her, Marissa realized the drink with Ansel was another thing she'd forgotten to tell him. She slid out of the car, hardly believing she was doing this. Breaking into Ansel Roche's car in broad daylight. She punched in the code. The door opened without a problem.

"Now what?" Riley asked, gazing into the empty interior.

Reaching over the passenger seat, she opened the glove compartment. Several scraps of paper flew out. "Now we're going to see if Roche keeps his diving gear in the car." She popped the latch that released the trunk lid.

Already around the car, Riley called out, "He does, all right."

Marissa was at his side in a second. Elated, she picked up the buoyancy compensator. "And he buys Predator equipment." Euphoria turned to sudden disappointment as she made a quick inspection of the gear. "But the shark is intact."

Riley dumped a pile of equipment back into the trunk. "Nothing else in here."

"Damn! I thought for sure . . ."

"Good try."

"Yeah, but now what? I'm sure it's Ansel. It all fits. His comforting Dori. His having some kind of heated confab with Glaser." When Riley gave her a black look, she defended herself. "I wasn't keeping it from you. I figured they were arguing about the resort bill or something. I'll bet they're in on this whole thing together."

"Then we'll find some other way of proving it," Riley assured her. "In the meantime, we'd better leave things as they were so Roche doesn't get suspicious."

"Right."

But as she leaned over the passenger seat to shut the glove compartment, she noticed the fallen slips of paper. She picked them up. Credit card receipts. She took a better look at the purchases. Gas. And the location and date. Her eyes widened.

"Riley," she said, hand shaking. When he didn't immediately respond, she called out again, more loudly. "Riley!"

"Your friend is otherwise occupied," came a familiar voice that did not belong to Riley O'Hare.

"Wha—!" Nerves ready to shatter, she twisted around.

Beyond Ansel Roche, who blocked her escape, she saw Riley, facedown on the pavement, blood oozing from the back of his head. Something swung into view.

"Looking for this?" Ansel asked.

Her eyes connected with a Predator weight belt . . . minus its shark insignia.

Chapter Thirteen

"You don't really think you're going to get away with this?"

Fear trailed icy fingers down Marissa's spine as Ansel Roche started the motor of the heretofore missing refuge skiff. Somehow he'd managed to collect and hide it. Riley was lying on the bottom, unconscious and trussed up tighter than she was. The circulation in her wrists was going, but at least her ankles remained free. Seeing that Ansel had a gun, she'd been forced to help him get Riley onto the yacht at Key Largo, where they'd waited until dark to leave. He'd come to once, several hours earlier, but Ansel had cold-bloodedly knocked him out again. Knowing how serious head injuries could be, she was worried sick about him.

"Everyone will believe O'Hare was responsible for those attempts on your life," Ansel was saying as he headed the skiff away from his yacht anchored in Florida Bay near the shallows, "and that you engaged in a life-and-death struggle that you both lost. Once I've returned to my yacht, I'll even send the skiff back in the direction where I leave you, so it will seem as if Riley had the boat all along."

Staring ahead into the dark, she said, "One problem with that plan."

"What's that?"

"No one knows that anyone was trying to kill me." No one but Detective Nick Lujan.

Ansel started. "Well, then, I'll see to it that people believe Riley killed Dori...and then you, to silence you, of course, once you figured it out. And before you tell me no one knows you were investigating, remember Viola Lynch. Knowing Dori's mother—wonderful, loyal woman that she is—she'd be delighted to testify to that fact. And to condemn the horrible bastard who got her girl pregnant, abandoned her and then killed the poor girl."

"But Riley didn't get her pregnant," Marissa ventured.

"Everyone believes he did."

"But you." They were sliding through back country, the shallows filled with uninhabited islands of black and red mangrove trees. Courtesy of the moon, she could make out silhouettes of the graceful roots clumping together to help in forming coastal lands. "You're the one, aren't you? Your comforting poor Dori went further than holding her hand."

"Mmm. My biggest regret at her death is that my child went with her. A man needs a son to cultivate, an heir to take over his kingdom when he's gone."

Wanting to know every detail in case they somehow got out of this alive, she asked, "Take over what?"

"The classiest, highest-priced resort in the keys. There won't be anything like it by the time I'm done. I've already bought one of the houses on the other side of the island, and I'm negotiating with the owner of the other. And don't worry about the dolphins.

They'll be part of the package, performing for people, swimming with them.''

The idea of his using marine mammals to further his nefarious plans sickened Marissa. In this situation, she'd rather see the animals freed than working for their supper.

"Overhearing Vida tell Glaser about O'Hare's father and their shaky land deal was the start of it all," Ansel went on. "I was sure if I could run O'Hare out of cash, I could get my hands on the land. The only kink in the plan is Toby Hanson. I'm not sure he'll sell. Of course, when he realizes the island will be loaded with tourists, he may come around fast.''

"And to think I suspected Hanson."

Ansel laughed. "He hasn't a clue, my dear.''

"But other people do.''

"Other people merely suspect.''

"You used them.''

"They were begging to be used. Vida, Glaser, even Dori.''

"What happened to Vida?" she asked, hearing an ominous sound—a heavy object slithering into a nearby channel. A crocodile?

She caught her breath as Ansel told her, "Last I heard, Vida hitched a ride to Key Largo, swearing she would never set foot on Lime Key again, but that she was going to get even with Riley for not giving her Dori's job if it was the last thing she ever did.''

Half-listening to Ansel, another part of her mind was remembering something she'd read recently about crocodiles. Though rarer than the freshwater alligator in the Everglades, the crocodiles that lurked in the briny channels were definitely more aggressive and potentially deadly. Forcing her thoughts back to the topic at hand, she said, "So Vida didn't know your plans."

"No one knows but Cole Glaser."

A twitch coming from the boat's bottom told her that either Riley was coming around or that he had been awake for some time and was merely reacting to the hated reporter's name.

Afraid of Ansel's reaction if he knew Riley was awake, she avoided looking down and instead asked, "Glaser's in on this with you?"

"Let's just say he was persuaded to cooperate at first by the lure of easy riches. Now he's terrified to cross me."

"Glaser can't reveal his part in this scheme without going to jail," Riley croaked, making her stomach fall. Why couldn't he keep his big mouth shut? But it seemed that Ansel was no longer worried about whether or not his nemesis was unconscious.

"And my threatening to sink him in the Gulf of Mexico with ballast attached to his legs helped his attitude along, as well," Ansel said gleefully. "Welcome back from your comatose state, O'Hare. You're just in time."

Marissa couldn't stop from asking herself, *In time for what?*

While Ansel turned his full attention to the complex channel, little more than a tortured winding through mangroves and hammocks, Marissa kept thinking of some way to escape. If only she could free herself and Riley, they could try to get away on foot. The channel was shallow and they might be able possibly to hide among the growth.

Riley groaned and shifted painfully.

"Not to worry," Ansel told him. "I'll see to your comfort very soon."

Fearing the exact nature of Ansel's intention, Marissa tried to distract him. "What about D'Angelo at Key Developers?"

"He knows only that I plan to buy the land when O'Hare defaults. But it was quite decent of him to have his girl call and warn me that you were snooping into the land deal."

"How did you get to Key Largo so fast?" Riley asked, making another feeble attempt to sit up.

"Simple. I was already anchored. I spoke to the gracious Miss Cavanaugh on the yacht phone." He gave a bored sigh. "Does that cover just about everything?"

"Just about." Remembering the slips she'd found in his glove compartment, she said, "Now if only Detective Lujan would think to look into your recent credit history, he'd find you bought gas for your car on the night of Dori's death . . . in Miami Beach."

"That was quite foolish of me not to fill the tank before leaving Key Largo," Ansel admitted, "but I don't think Lujan will have just cause to get a court order to look into my personal records, so I think I'm safe there."

"So you drove to Miami Beach, knowing where the refuge boat would stop to refuel," Riley said. "Then you knocked Ken out, left him tied up, and forced Dori to take the boat out, where you choked her until she was unconscious, then threw her overboard."

"After sleeping with her," Marissa said, in case Riley hadn't heard that part. "Even if you didn't know about *your baby*, didn't you care about her at all?"

"I liked her well enough, but she found out my plans for the refuge. If the blackmail didn't work, I had other ways in mind of ruining the operation. Dori was sleeping with me, but she was still loyal to O'Hare. She threatened to expose me if I didn't back off.''

"My father will never sell to you," Riley said.

"Ward Strong will be deliriously happy to rid himself of that land and the potential embarrassment it could bring him."

"You don't know Father. He doesn't embarrass. At all."

"Too bad." Ansel punctuated his statement by cutting the motor. While the boat continued drifting, he removed two weapons from his jacket pockets—a knife and a gun. He waved the second at Marissa. "Over here."

A nearby splash, louder than the first, sent a chill through her. They were definitely in crocodile waters and she didn't like it.

Heart pounding, she drew closer to Ansel, knowing he had to cut her bonds. He couldn't very well stage the drama he'd described if both she and Riley were hog-tied. His very nearness made her flesh crawl, and she hated to turn her back on him. But turn she did, and within seconds she felt the sharp blade cut through the ropes around her wrists.

"Now you can do the same for O'Hare," he said, holding the knife handle toward her as she turned back to face him. He edged the gun into her sight. "Don't try anything foolish."

She took the knife and was tempted, anyway. "How about filling in the details?" she asked, using the weapon to free Riley as Ansel had demanded.

"I thought about feeding you to the sharks, but that's kind of a hit-or-miss proposition. The crocodiles will do quite nicely. The knife please, handle first."

Complying, she laughed. "You don't know much about wild animals, do you? Crocodiles are not as bloodthirsty as you imagine."

"These may be," Riley said tensely.

She gave him a seething look, which she was certain he couldn't see in the dark. "Not necessarily."

"So you've heard of Moony Tucker, have you, O'Hare?"

"Who?" Marissa asked.

Easing into a sitting position, Riley groaned. "He's a lunatic who brings his beer buddies out here to toss road kill to the crocs. They have a rip-roarin', good ol' time watching the feeding frenzy when the crocs catch the scent of blood."

Horrified, Marissa looked around disbelievingly. Was that a log floating just a few feet away in the channel? Or was it a crocodile?

"You can't be serious," she whispered, staring at Ansel.

"Oh, but I am. There might not be enough left of either of you to identify, but not every plan can be perfect." He let that sink in and added, "Oh, yes, for the plan to work, it will help if you are both bleeding when you go into the water."

He lashed out with the knife and scored the tip along Marissa's arm. Blood spurted and she screamed. Riley lunged toward the villain, who calmly fired the gun.

"God, no!" she yelled both in pain and terror as Riley's body jerked and collapsed.

He groaned and spit out, "Flesh wound. Leg." And grabbed his thigh as if to stop the bleeding.

Marissa felt a warm wetness ooze down her arm through the material of her jacket. "You're crazy, Ansel. You're a lunatic."

Ansel laughed until the boat came to an abrupt stop, sliding into a mud bank. "Damn!"

Slithering noises cut through the suddenly still night. Growing faint from the knife wound, Marissa gave herself a mental shake. If she didn't think quickly, it would be all over. Riley was sitting up again, but his face was a mask of pain. He probably couldn't rely on that leg, and who knew what kind of shape his head was in after being whacked twice. If they had any chance of escape, it lay with her.

"You're stuck now," she said. "Toss us over the side and you'll be surrounded. I've heard crocs can jump to get their prey."

Ansel cursed. "The push pole. Find it."

Marissa smothered the smile that tempted her lips, even though she doubted he could see it in nothing more than the moonlight. "What if I don't?"

"What if I shoot your lover here again?"

The temptation to smile vanished. "All right, all right, I'll get it."

Kicking off her heels, she moved closer to Riley and felt along the bottom of the skiff. He gave her a look of determination—as if he meant to do something brave and foolish to save them. Eyes wide, she shook her head, praying he would take heed and give up the control-freak thing just this once. Her hand finally came in contact with the pole, which was ten feet long and had a spatulate end that could be used to push them off the mud bank.

"Got it," she said softly, giving Riley another warning look.

A glowering expression wreathed his face, but he inclined his head slightly.

"Well, what are you waiting for?" Ansel demanded. "Use it."

She gauged her distance from him to be about eight feet. Shoving the push pole into the mud bank, she took a few minutes to carefully work the skiff free. Then, giving the boat her most powerful shove in hopes that the backward movement would throw Ansel off balance, she flew around on the attack, aiming the spatulate end of the push pole at his throat.

Bull's-eye!

With a gurgle, Ansel threw his hands up . . . and dropped the gun. And just as quickly, Riley dived for the weapon.

"Son of a bitch!" the villain growled low. His knife hand arced downward.

Marissa struck out again, cracking his left wrist so hard, she swore she heard it break. The knife flipped over the side, making a big splash.

As did something else. Something made an even bigger splash. Something equally deadly. And alive. The hairs on the back of her neck stood straight up as Marissa imagined hearing similar sounds issuing from several different directions at once.

And before her, a life-and-death struggle was being played out as the two men wrestled for the gun. Ansel was in good shape, while Riley was wounded. Desperation might give one strength, but Marissa despaired that Riley, in his weakened condition, was no match for the felon. She waited for her moment and struck out, but this time Ansel ducked . . . and her momentum sent her flying right out of the boat.

"Marissa!" Riley yelled.

Don't panic! she told herself yet again, as she landed in the barely waist-deep water.

The menacing sounds of creatures that could be as big as twelve feet in length steadily drifted closer. And she could not get a foothold to properly right herself as the boat drifted away. The marly bottom of the channel was sucking at her feet, which sank deeper and deeper as she struggled to catch up to the boat. Visions of quicksand entered her head, though she knew the bottom was merely sucky, sticky stuff that squished between her toes and edged up to her ankles.

Sucky and sticky enough to get her killed. For from every direction, it seemed a rough-barked log glided closer. She knew these were no felled trees but creatures that some lunatic had trained with road kill. Well, bleeding or not, she was no road kill. She was alive and intended to stay that way. Anchoring the push pole in the marl, she pulled her feet upward, then shoved herself toward the boat with all her remaining strength.

Flying across the shallow water, Marissa hit the metal side with her wounded arm. She saw stars and gasped with pain.

"Marissa, I'll get you!"

Somehow Riley had managed to wrest the gun from Ansel and was now crawling along the bottom of the skiff to reach her. The snap of jaws behind her was incentive enough to make her walk on water if she could. With a big heave, ignoring the tearing pain caused by the cut, Marissa managed to get her upper half over the side, making the boat pitch. Riley latched onto her clothing and pulled. She clenched her jaw and helped.

Behind Riley, Ansel rose, flashlight in hand like a club. Marissa heaved again, throwing her legs into the skiff hard, purposely rocking it. Startled, Ansel threw out his hands to balance himself. Quickly clutching a handful of discarded rope, Marissa flung it in his face.

Ansel's reaction was a sharp jerk that began the momentum he couldn't stop.

"No-o-o!" he yelled as he tumbled over the side, limbs flailing.

Marissa couldn't distinguish his splash from the sound of others. Grateful that they were both still alive, she threw herself at Riley, whose arms wound around her back and held her tight. She closed her eyes and imagined he did, too.

Churning and snapping, the crocodiles closed in for the kill.

DAYLIGHT CREPT ALONG the screened-in porch of the Florida house, and Billie was lifting the covers from the bird cages at the far end. Marissa and Riley were just finishing up answering all of Detective Nick Lujan's questions.

"Doesn't seem likely that we're going to find much evidence of Ansel Roche himself."

A shiver sped through Marissa as she remembered waiting, seemingly endlessly, for the feeding frenzy to die down enough for them to leave the area. Sitting with her on the sofa, Riley tightened the hold he had on her hand.

"Roche got what he deserved."

"Riley!"

"If he'd managed to kill you, I would've torn him apart with my bare teeth."

"Right," she said grimly. "You were in perfect shape to do it, too."

A quick trip to a Key Largo clinic had already confirmed that Riley would easily survive both the flesh wound from the bullet and the blows to the head. And while Marissa's arm ached where several stitches held the knife wound together beneath the bandages, she didn't resent the reminder that she was definitely, vividly alive.

"How soon can you come down to my office to go through your statements again?" Lujan wanted to know.

"You've got to be kidding!" Riley groused.

Marissa placed a firm finger across his lips. "Will tomorrow afternoon be soon enough?"

"You got it." Packing away his notebook in the pocket of his rumpled alligator-print shirt—the very sight of which made her shudder—Lujan started to leave. He paused at the screen door, saying, "Forget the hard-line stuff I read you the other day, Miss Gilmore. You ever want to change your occupation, you come see me."

No sooner had he disappeared from view than Riley asked, "Would you?"

"Would I what?"

"Want to change your occupation?"

Wondering if he could possibly be asking her what she thought he was asking, she said, "It never occurred to me."

"Let it."

Heart suddenly thumping out of excitement rather than fear for once, she demanded, "Okay, explain."

"I thought maybe you'd consider applying for Dori's job."

"Oh." *Disappointed!*

"Hmm, I get the feeling that that didn't come out right," he said, renewing her hope. "I cared about Dori, and obviously I wronged her, but I never loved her the way I do you. I have a vacancy—"

"Vacancy?" He'd better do this right.

"Damn it, woman, I want you to work with me."

Better. "What's the incentive?"

"Helping me build Dolphin Haven into the best marine mammal refuge in the world."

"That takes money, and you're not willing to do what's necessary to make it."

"I could have a change of heart about the public relations stuff . . . if the reward was big enough."

"What are we talking about here?"

"A lifetime commitment."

"Working in the refuge."

"By my side."

"What's the incentive?" she stubbornly asked again.

He kissed her tenderly. "That's one incentive." Passionately. "Another." Aggressively. "I could keep doing this until one of us runs out of air."

Breathing hard, she said, "We don't have to use up our entire air supply all at once, do we?"

"Actually, I was thinking about spreading it over a whole lifetime."

"That's better," she murmured, offering her lips again.

He claimed them only until they were interrupted by the clearing of a throat.

Marissa pulled free and turned her head. "Erasmus. And Luke." Her heart sank when she remembered the boy's reaction the last time he'd found her in his father's arms.

"Hey, you guys well enough to be doing that stuff?" Luke asked with a smirk.

Marissa relaxed.

The grizzled fisherman grinned at them as he strode onto the porch. "Congratulations in order?"

"Why?" Riley asked. "You planning on reporting back to my father?"

The grin slipped into a nervous tick. "Your, uh, what?"

"That's what you've been doing, isn't it? Spying on me for him?"

Decidedly uncomfortable, Erasmus cleared his throat again. "Well, I wouldn't put it that way."

"Then how would you put it?"

"I been making sure he knows how you're doing . . . since you won't."

Riley frowned. "If he was so damn interested, why didn't he ask me himself?"

"Guess you two are too much alike," Billie piped up from where she'd been hovering in the background.

Marissa snorted.

"Don't say it," Riley warned her.

Certain he meant the control-freak thing, she held herself back. "Maybe it's time Ward Strong and Riley O'Hare started acting like father and son."

"She's pretty smart, Dad. You oughta listen to her," Luke said, a note of hope in his voice.

"He wouldn't have it unless I toed his line."

"You're wrong," Erasmus said. "He'll take you any way he can get you . . . not that he'd say as much. Too stubborn. And he could use you right now, what with all the trouble his company is in."

Rather than saying something derogatory about Marathon Fisheries and the Ocean Watch lawsuit, Riley said, "I'll think about it."

"He'll do something about it," Marissa promised for him, disbelieving that Riley could possibly be happy estranged from his father as he'd been for the past dozen years.

Then Billie broke in. "Luke . . . Erasmus . . . I could use some help getting breakfast out on the deck."

Grumbling, fisherman and teenager followed the housekeeper out.

No sooner were they out of sight than Riley demanded, "You think you can tell me what to do?"

"Unless you hate your father that much?" His expression told her he didn't. "Besides, fair's fair."

He moved in closer, giving her one of those threatening looks that thrilled her down to her toes. "Then you'd better have a lifelong claim on me. As I was saying before we were so rudely interrupted, I want you by my side professionally...and personally. You've already made one lifetime commitment to your work and—"

"I accept."

He ceased midargument. "You do?"

"Let's go tell the kids the good news." And she didn't mean Luke.

Within minutes, they stood before the dolphin enclosure, announcing their love to the intelligent creatures who for the moment depended on them, but who, hopefully, would one day be as safe and as free as Marissa was in her heart. For finally, she'd found a man with whom she could share not only the rest of her life but all of her passions.

With the dolphins dancing in what she imagined was delight for their happiness, Marissa hugged Riley's side, the silent sea spreading out before them as endless as she hoped their love would be.

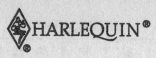

WEDDING SONG
Vicki Lewis Thompson

Kerry Muldoon has encountered more than her share of happy brides and grooms. She and her band—the Honeymooners—play at all the wedding receptions held in romantic Eternity, Massachusetts!

Kerry longs to walk down the aisle one day— with sexy recording executive Judd Roarke. But Kerry's dreams of singing stardom threaten to tear apart the fragile fabric of their union....

WEDDING SONG, available in August from Temptation, is the third book in Harlequin's new cross-line series, **WEDDINGS, INC.** Be sure to look for the fourth book, **THE WEDDING GAMBLE,** by Muriel Jensen (Harlequin American Romance #549), coming in September.

WED3